W9-AYS-755

Hating Alison Ashley

By the same author

Games ...
Boss of the Pool
Halfway Across the Galaxy
People Might Hear You
Laurie Loved Me Best

Robin Klein

Hating Alison Ashley

Published by The Trumpet Club
a division of Bantam Doubleday Dell Publishing Group, Inc.
666 Fifth Avenue, New York, New York 10103

ISBN: 0-440-84298-0

Reprinted by arrangement with Viking Penguin,
a division of Penguin Books USA Inc.
Printed in the United States of America
September 1990

10 9 8 7 6 5 4 3 2 1
OPM

For Jill Cantor

ONE

I will never forgive my mother for calling me Erica with a surname like Yurken.

When an emergency teacher was taking our grade (we got a lot of emergency teachers at our school because the ordinary ones were often away with nervous problems), the emergency teacher would say something like, 'Girl in the end row with the dark hair, what's your name?' But before I could answer, kids would screech out 'Erk!' Or 'Yuk!' Or 'Gherkin!' Except Barry Hollis who always yelled out something worse, but emergency teachers were given a counselling session by the Principal before they came into our room, so they knew enough to pretend not to hear Barry Hollis.

Erk, Yuk, or Gherkin. When I grew up and left school and left Barringa East for ever, I planned to change my name to something really elegant. It was a waste of time doing it before then. Elegance just didn't fit in Barringa East, which was what is known as a socially disadvantaged area.

1

Mum sometimes said we ought to move out of Barringa East to somewhere a bit more posh, but she really quite liked living there. She said she'd even got used to the sound of the police sirens chasing after the Eastside Boys late at night, though they didn't seem to have much luck catching them.

The Eastside Boys were the big brothers of the kids at our school. They wrote their name with spray paint everywhere: Eastside Boys Wuz Here. It was written all over the footpaths and on the waiting-room ceiling at the station, and on our school tuckshop when it was busted into. It even got into the local papers: 'Eastside Boys Go On Rampage Through Shopping Centre' or 'Eastside Boys Brawl at Skating Rink – Manager and Staff Barricade Themselves in Office'.

'In spite of the Eastside Boys, there's advantages about living here,' mum said.

'Name just one,' I said bitterly.

'Well, Barringa East Primary School for a start,' she said. 'You ought to be grateful, Erk. What about all those nice things the government bought for that little school?'

That was because Barringa East Primary was classified as a Disadvantaged School. The kids weren't supposed to know it was called that in case they got a complex. I only found out because I spent a lot of time in the temporary sick bay, which was between the secretary's office and the staff room. The walls were made of thin masonite sheets. The Eastside Boys had burned down a couple of classrooms and the proper sick bay, so everything was cramped and partitioned until funds came through for rebuilding.

Because our school was classified as being Disadvantaged, we were given all this equipment, such as a photography dark-room, two table-tennis tables, lots of excursions we didn't have to bring money from home for, and an annual camp for grade six.

The grade-six teacher at Barringa East Primary was Miss Belmont. She was terrifying, but very stylish. She had a lovely figure, and her hair was silvery grey tipped with blonde streaks. Her face was smooth and tanned because she played a lot of sport. She didn't smoke, so her teeth looked like television-ad teeth. I liked carrying her bag from her car each morning because both were expensive looking, and I liked to pretend that they belonged to me.

She could keep a class in order better than anyone else in the whole school. She could even squash Barry Hollis. The reason she was given grade six was because Mr Kennard told the Principal he would resign and get a job on the Council garbage truck rather than take our class. (That was one of the things I heard through the masonite walls in the sick bay.) Although she was a dictator, Miss Belmont had some admirable qualities. The first day of the term she said, 'Dark-haired girl in the end row, what's your name?' and everyone did their thing about Erk, Yuk and Gherkin.

Miss Belmont glanced coldly from one yelling

face to the next, right round the room, and that glance was as effective as a series of sharp slaps. The faces stopped yelling one by one, like falling dominoes. Even Barry Hollis kicked the desk in front of him more quietly.

I said with dignity that my name was Erica Yurken.

'Erica's a very nice name,' Miss Belmont said. 'It means "great heroine".'

'It means . . .' said Barry Hollis, and gave his own personal definition

'And what's YOUR name, young man?' Miss Belmont asked. 'Barry Hollis, is it? Right, I've committed it to memory, Barry Hollis, AND IF YOU DON'T STOP KICKING THAT DESK THERE IS GOING TO BE A HOLE IN THE WINDOW PANE EXACTLY YOUR SIZE AND SHAPE IN THE NEXT THREE SECONDS!'

It sounded weird, a voice that fierce and immense coming out of such a ladylike teacher. Even her hair looked violent, as though it would send off a shower of electric sparks. Everyone sat as still and quiet as new Derwent pencils in a box.

'That's more like it,' Miss Belmont purred. 'Now we'll do some WORK!'

Usually on the first day of a term people romp light-heartedly around the room and fights break out about who's sitting where and the teacher tears her hair and fusses about timetables and maths books and such. But Miss Belmont had all that

4

organized before school even started, and you'd never believe the work we got through that first morning.

She seemed to have eyes like a fly, with multiple sections that could see sideways and backwards, and into things that hadn't even happened yet. Such as into Barry Hollis's desk where he had a packet of cigarettes and a copy of *Playboy*.

By the morning recess we all had writer's cramp and mental exhaustion, but Miss Belmont looked quite calm and relaxed as she sailed into the staff room for coffee. I'd never cared to associate with the riff-raff in the playground at Barringa East Primary. I went into the office and asked Mrs Orlando, the school secretary, if I could lie down during recess because I had a headache. On my medical card in the office it said I was prone to nervous headaches, rhinitis, sinusitis, bee-sting allergy, rheumatism; suspected hypersensitivity to wattle pollen, horsehair, dust mite, clover and Clag glue; tested for diabetes, arthritis, gallstones and hiatus hernia; and that I didn't have to put my head under water when we went swimming because of a punctured eardrum. Mum didn't write all that information on the sheet they'd sent home for parents to fill in; I'd supplied it to Mrs Orlando over the six years I'd been going to Barringa East Primary.

Mrs Orlando said I could lie down during recess, but that I had to go straight back to class when the bell rang. She didn't sound all that sympathetic. She always looked as though you were a nuisance, even

5

if you just wanted a band-aid, because she had to leave her typewriter and fetch the key to open the first-aid cupboard in the sick bay. The key was kept on a nail high up, under the office ceiling, ever since Barry Hollis pinched everything out of the first-aid cupboard and sold it to the Eastside Boys for gang warfare medical supplies. The sick bay was my favourite place at school. It was exciting to lie hunched up and groan and pretend that your appendix had just burst when kids stickybeaked in through the window. And also, it was the best place in the school for gaining classified information.

When Mrs Orlando went back into her office, I put my ear to the wall. She wasn't saying anything particularly newsworthy, only, 'That pest of a Yuk is just as neurotic as ever.'

The new grade-two teacher who had crept in there to ask what she should do about the dirty big hole someone kicked in her class-room door, said, 'Who on earth is Yuk?' New teachers at our school always seemed to creep around looking pale and stricken for their first few weeks.

Mrs Orlando said, 'Erica Yurken, the school hypochondriac.' (It's always interesting to listen to people talking about you behind your back.)

Mrs Orlando got on with her typing. She always had a lot of it, because Mr Nicholson, the Principal, was a workaholic. Which means that he threw himself into work like someone hurling themselves off a cliff. He seemed to stay in his office a lot, with the door shut, and if you sneaked up and peered in through the window from the outside, he sometimes had his head in his hands and a glass of water and a packet of Quick-Eze on his desk. He probably found that being the Principal of Barringa East Primary was daunting.

I put my ear to the staff-room wall. They were all going on about what they did in their holidays, and their boyfriends – except the new teachers who didn't seem to be saying anything. Maybe they had their heads in their hands, too. 'How are you getting on with grade six, Helen?' someone asked Miss Belmont.

'How do you mean?' she asked.

'All those ratty kids in that grade, how come it's so quiet up your end of the corridor?'

'They've been working quite well,' she said. 'I'm not having any trouble. Why should I?'

Then I couldn't listen to anything else because this wailing little kid came in with a bump on his head the size of a cantaloupe where Barry Hollis had donged him with a triangular carton of frozen orange juice. Miss Belmont marched into the sick bay to see what the noise was about. When she saw me in bed, she said, 'Out you go, Erica, into the fresh air if you've got a headache.' And to the bawling little kid she said, 'Stop that ridiculous noise. There's no need to make such a fuss about a small bump on the head. And what do you mean, will this antiseptic sting? Of course it will sting, and you're quite old enough to cope with pain.' And to Barry Hollis, lounging about in the doorway where he'd been dragged by the teacher on playground duty, she said, 'Wait outside the office until Mr Nicholson finishes his morning tea. Erica, be gone by the time I count one.'

So I couldn't find out if he got detention or not, though Mr Nicholson didn't keep him in very often because every time he did, Barry Hollis's big brother in the Eastside Boys would come to school after dark and rip up shrubs or break windows. Barry stuck his foot out automatically to trip me up, but he did that to everyone, and you developed good swerving reflexes. Luckily he wasn't at school all that much, only on an average of three days a week. The rest of the time he travelled. He went to all sorts of places, and had seen more of Victoria than my mum's new boyfriend, who was a truck driver. Only Barry went by train without paying.

When I got home from school that first day, I took my secret theatre notebook out from under my mattress. The sole ambition of my life was to become a famous actress. The notebook was a sort of teach-yourself training manual. I wrote down all the memorable things Miss Belmont had said that day.

Then I practised saying them aloud in her voice. I don't want to seem boastful, but I got it absolutely perfect the first try; tone, pitch, everything. There was no doubt whatsoever that I was destined for a glittering, brilliant career in the theatre.

That's if I ever managed to escape from Barringa East.

TWO

People outside the area gave you funny looks when you told them you lived in Barringa East. Mum had never stayed married long enough to save up for a house elsewhere. She received a social security pension, and also a wage from her part-time job as a barmaid, but she didn't tell the government about that in case she lost her pension. Which meant that she was lying to them, even though she was always going mad at me for lying, except in my case I thought of it as decorating statements to make them sound more interesting.

Besides me in our family, there was my big brother Harley and my two sisters, Valjoy and Jedda. (Mum had a weird taste in names.) Harley left school two years ago. He'd been looking for a job ever since, only he didn't really look all that hard.

'How come they haven't found you a job yet down at that Commonwealth Employment Office?' mum demanded. 'What did you tell them, that you were an out-of-work admiral, or a taxidermist, for heaven's sake! What about that telegram they sent on Monday?'

'I went out for the interview,' said Harley, sly as a swagman's kelpie.

'So what happened?'

'My foot stuck in this grating thing by the factory door, and they had to find a metal cutter. And by that time a hundred other kids queued up and got interviewed.'

'Let's see the bruise, then.'

'Haven't got one. It was an old bit of grating all covered in soft moss.'

Harley liked loafing in his hammock studying books about astral projection. That means you can make your spirit leave your physical body and move around without anyone knowing. Harley had this idea that if he could train himself to do that, he might be able to get a really interesting highly paid job as a spy or detective. And he wouldn't have to leave his hammock to go to work, either.

Mum said it was a lot of creepy nonsense, and who in their right mind would want to leave their bodies and float around like wisps of smoke? There wasn't anything smoky about mum. She really enjoyed being alive, and getting dressed up to go out. She went to Bingo nights, and dances, and Tupperware parties, and Parents Without Partners, which was where she met Lennie, who was her new boyfriend. Valjoy said she had a nerve joining Parents Without Partners when she'd already had two partners and a whole lot of boyfriends as well.

Valjoy was named after mum's two sisters, but she hated them both because they were always telling mum if they saw her hanging around the pizza parlour with any of the Eastside Boys. She said she wished her name was Danielle or Monique, but the crowd she hung round with didn't ever call each other by their proper names, anyhow. Everyone in that crowd wore black t-shirts, with their nicknames on the front in iron-on vinyl letters. They all had names like Spook, Blonk, Dagger, Scum, Dracula, and Titch, and Valjoy's nickname in that crowd was Curves.

Mum went mad every time Valjoy wore that black t-shirt saying Curves, but Valjoy had a worse one hidden away, which she sneaked out for parties. It had 'I can be very, very friendly' written across the front.

Valjoy was fifteen and still at Tech but she was planning to leave at the end of the year and become a motor mechanic or a boilermaker. She said it was dumb to go into an office job where you'd only meet hundreds of other girls. You'd have more fun if you were, for instance, the only girl driving a crane with a firm that employed twenty other crane drivers, all fellers.

Valjoy was sort of boy mad.

Then there was my little sister Jedda. Jedda was sort of horse mad. Although she was already six, she went round wearing a tail made out of plaited pantyhose pinned to the back of her jeans. She was utterly embarrassing, and I had to share a bedroom with her. She made stables out of the furniture on her side of the room and slept in them instead of in her proper bed. She ate in there, too, which I didn't think was very hygienic. There was always a long line of ants parading across the bedroom floor after Jedda's left-over jam sandwiches and soggy cornflakes, But mum never ticked her off about it.

Valjoy wouldn't let me in her room and I wouldn't have wanted to share a room with her, anyway. When she was in a bad mood, it was like being with a dangerous animal with a thorn in its paw. Also, she learned martial arts, another way she figured she might meet boys, but she said it was a real let down, because that karate centre was full of nice polite Asian university students who were so brainy she couldn't understand what they were talking about. I was careful not to annoy her since she started learning martial arts. She said she knew how to paralyse people for life, just by using her elbow.

As though our house wasn't already small and noisy enough, Lennie was always dropping in for meals. He had this great, clanging, bumper-bar voice. Every time he came out with some unfunny remark, which I personally thought more polite to pretend he never said, mum would shriek and fall about laughing.

It was always bedlam at our house. Valjoy was forever slamming out of the front door hollering that she was going, this time for good, and not to expect her home ever again. And mum would yell after her that it was the best news she'd heard since she won the fridge in the football-club raffle and good riddance – only she didn't ever mean it. And in the background Jedda would be whinnying or watching the TV racing results with the sound turned up full blast. She knew all the names of race horses and their trainers. I didn't think it was very elegant at all that a little kid understood how the TAB betting system worked, but mum and Lennie egged her on.

'Call a race for us, love,' mum would say, and Jedda would start chanting, 'Irish Mist getting a clear run on the rails, followed by Uranus, King Herod sneaking up on the outside, followed by Percy Boy, followed by Champagne Charley, with Sky's the Limit and Take a Gamble well back in the field . . .'

Yet our house wasn't as unrefined as some of the others in the street. As a matter of fact, we had some pretty peculiar neighbours. Nobody sat in judgement over anyone else in Barringa East because they had too many skeletons in their own cupboards.

Mrs Pegg next door had a lot of travelling expenses. She had to visit her son Terry who was in a home in the country for uncontrollable teenagers because he liked driving. He didn't have a licence or a car of his own, so he borrowed other people's without asking. The first time he did that, they let him out under the supervision of a parole officer, but he borrowed the parole officer's VW without asking and drove off to Perth.

The family on the other side of us were threatened with eviction because they didn't pay the rent. They nailed boards across the windows and doors and barricaded themselves in with a supply of tinned food. It was even exciting for a while, seeing who would win, but mum felt sorry for Mrs Mac-Mahon and went down to the real-estate office and paid all the back rent out of the $300 she'd saved up for a fur coat.

'You're crazy,' Valjoy said. 'She'll never pay it back. And what if social security finds out you had all that money stashed away for a fur coat? Pensioners aren't supposed to go around wearing fur coats. One day you'll get sprung about that hotel job.'

'I'll worry about that when it happens,' said mum. 'Lennie said he'd buy me a fur, anyhow, the day I make up my mind to marry him. What kind do you reckon, Valjoy? That pale goldy-colour fur, or dark, or something really eye catching, like red fox?'

That was the only time she and Valjoy ever had nice quiet conversations, when they discussed clothes that hadn't been bought yet.

Barringa East was a messy patchwork sort of place. The people who actually owned their houses had done them up nicely with sunblinds and gardens, and the ones who had moved out from high-rise flats usually went to a lot of trouble, too, because they were so glad to move into a place with a front and back yard. But a lot of no-hopers also lived in Barringa East, and it was depressing walking along some of those streets past houses that looked like decaying fruit. They had newspapers pasted up instead of curtains; waist-high weeds for a garden, and skinny bitzer dogs guarding nothing. And the driveways were full of old cars that had died.

Barringa East wasn't very large. You could walk from one end of it to the other in twenty minutes, even allowing for detours to avoid Barry Hollis who was usually out hunting for someone to pick on. On all four sides of Barringa East there was a main road, as though it had been set on purpose into a frame. It was really peculiar. Outside the frame were the smart suburbs, with new brick houses and double garages holding shiny big cars and speed-boats on trailers.

Those suburbs had their own schools and they weren't a bit like Barringa East Primary. Some-times, only not very often because we weren't invited all that much, our netball and football teams played theirs. Their kids didn't yell and swear at the umpire like the kids in our teams, or turn round and beat each other up for missing the ball.

Our local paper was always printing news items about those schools. There'd be photographs with captions underneath: 'Gilland Primary School raised $200 for the Seeing Eye Dog Centre by making and selling pottery.' 'Edgeworth Primary had a most exciting day coming to school dressed as their favourite book characters.' 'Four students from Jacana Heights Primary have won scholarships to Bloggs Grammar School and Moggs Ladies College.'

The only time I remember our school being mentioned in that paper was when the classrooms burned down and the heading was 'Arson Suspected at Barringa East Primary'.

But while I was in sixth grade, they built a new freeway – and one of the roads that was part of the framework for keeping Barringa East in its place was divided. This little section of Hedge End Road, only three or four houses long, suddenly found itself plonked officially onto the end of Barringa East, like a satin rosette stuck on a packet of fish and chips. And the school zoning system meant that anyone who lived in that cut-off bit of Hedge End Road had to send their kids to Barringa East Primary School.

However, there wasn't a great rush of new enrolments to our school. Maybe the owners of those big houses became rich by not having kids, or maybe they felt so disgusted at being officially part of Barringa East that they moved.

But there was one kid, Alison Ashley, and she started at Barringa East Primary two weeks after the beginning of first term. Maybe it took her parents a whole fortnight to recover from the shock that she had to come to our crummy school. But when she did arrive, because no one was sitting next to me, Miss Belmont put Alison Ashley there.

And from the first day I hated her.

THREE

She was wearing this soft blue skirt, and a shirt the colour of cream, with not a crease nor a wrinkle nor a loose thread anywhere. Expensive-looking plaited leather sandals. Long, pale gold hair caught back with a filagree clasp, and tiny gold roses, the size of shirt buttons, in her ears. Her skin was tanned and each cheek had a deep, soft dimple. Huge navy-blue eyes, the colour of ink, fringed with dark curly lashes. She was the most beautiful, graceful, elegant thing you ever saw in your life.

A hush lapped right round our classroom when Mrs Orlando brought her in and introduced her to Miss Belmont. The hush didn't last very long; Barry Hollis jammed his fingers in his mouth and made ape noises, and that set off all the boys in the back row. Miss Belmont just froze them into silence with her iceberg-that-sunk-the-*Titanic* look, and then she told Alison to sit next to me. 'Erica will show you around the school and look after you till you settle in, Alison,' she said.

Alison opened the lid of her side of the desk and

began to put her things away. It seemed almost insulting to call them things. She had a gold biro with a short chain on the end, and on the end of the chain was a little gold A. She had a pencil case made of gold leather with her initials in one corner. Her work folder looked brand new. It was covered with beautiful grey and white marbled paper, and she opened it to a new page and ruled a perfect margin with her little gold biro. Then she rested her hands on the page and looked politely at Miss Belmont.

I glanced at her nails. They had white crescent moons at the base with all the cuticles pushed back, and every nail was a perfect shell-pink oval. Alison Ashley impressed me to such a degree that I wanted her to know immediately that there was at least one person at Barringa East Primary who was, like herself, a tall flower in a garden full of couch grass and weeds.

'I just adore your earrings,' I whispered. 'I'd like to have my ears pierced, only I'm allergic to methylated spirits. So I guess I'll have to go to a dermatologist and have him supervise the post-operative care. You can't be too careful, even for a minor operation like ear piercing. My sister Valjoy offered to do it for nothing with a compass point, but I certainly don't want to end up with blood poisoning. When I get my ears pierced, it's going to be in a proper sterilized operating theatre by a qualified surgeon. I already have a very nice pair of earrings at home soaking in a bowl of antiseptic.

I chose them myself. They're little squirrels holding baskets of nuts.'

Alison Ashley didn't say anything, but she raised her eyebrows slightly. Her eyebrows were like fine brush strokes in a Japanese print. I realized suddenly that there was a silence in the room, and Miss Belmont was standing by the blackboard with the chalk in her hand, and her eyebrows were raised, too, but they didn't look like delicate Japanese brush strokes. They looked like fierce arrows.

I hastily copied down the notes she'd made on the blackboard about open-cut coal mining, which was not a topic I found interesting. It had no bearing whatever on a career in the theatre. My writing, which was very highly strung and filled with nervous energy, jerked all over the paper. My whole folder, to tell the truth, was a mess. I'd covered it with Superman gift-wrapping paper which seemed now, next to Alison's folder, extremely juvenile. All the spaces between the repeated motifs of Superman going Pow! and Zap! were scribbled on. I scribbled compulsively, and the result looked like some really repulsive, spreading fungus.

I peeped at Alison's immaculate work, and began to feel a tiny bit inferior. It was a new and upsetting emotion for me, as ever since I set foot in Barringa East Primary way back in prep grade, I had always felt totally superior to every single person in the whole school, including the Principal, and also the District Inspector when he came around.

We finished the work about coal mines and Miss Belmont asked some brisk, sneaky questions around the room, to trap kids like Barry Hollis who hadn't been paying attention. The questions were hard, so she received blank looks from everyone. But when she asked Alison, Alison answered correctly. And it was like that right up to lunch break. Alison Ashley knew all her tables and got all her maths right. She turned out to have a reading age of 14.6 years. She knew all the rivers of northern New South Wales in perfect order.

My feelings of inferiority swelled into dislike, and the dislike into absolute loathing. I was so sick with jealous resentment that I could hardly even bear to open my order from the tuckshop. Mum often let me buy my lunch because she hated cutting school lunches. She said it wrecked her nail varnish. I'd ordered a meat pie, an iced jam donut, and this lovely big yellow banana, just begging to be unzipped and eaten.

Miss Belmont wouldn't let us talk while we ate our lunches. You could hear the fifth grade next door racketing around in their room and yelling, and every now and then their teacher (Mr Kennard, the one who said he'd resign if he was given our class) roared desperately, 'QUIET! Stop carrying on like a zoo! Who poured tomato sauce into this box of paper clips?'

But Miss Belmont just sat tidily with a straight back and all she had to do was let her eye fall thoughtfully on anyone who belched or acted like a zoo, and they changed their minds.

I looked sideways at Alison Ashley's lunch. She had it in a white plastic lunchbox with little compartments. In one compartment she had a chicken drumstick wrapped in foil. In another she had a stick of celery with the tips curled (I found out later how you do that, you slice it and stand it in iced water), a tiny perfect tomato like a ruby, a baby carrot and two cheese sticks, all cuddled up on a lettuce leaf so crisp you could have used it as a get-well card.

Alison Ashley had a slice of wholemeal bread with the butter spread evenly right up to every crust, and a smart white drink bottle with a gold lid, filled with orange juice. She also had a straw in a cellophane wrap. She ate so quietly and nicely that you couldn't hear her chew, not even when she got to the celery. When she finished her lunch, she shook crumbs that didn't exist onto the spread-out foil and put it into the bin. She replaced the lids on her white lunchbox and her white drink bottle and put them both away in her school bag.

When the bell rang for everyone to go outside and play, there was the usual stampede from Mr Kennard's grade, and the sound of him dragging his feet along to the staff room for his own lunch, whimpering softly to himself. But we all sat at our desks until Miss Belmont said 'All right, Grade Six, you may go out.'

Alison Ashley looked at me and waited.

'I'm supposed to show you round the school,' I said grittily. 'So come on.'

First, I showed her the library, because it was the only modern room and had been designed by an architect. Probably by an architect who read our local paper, because whenever our school was broken into, which was just about every second weekend, the library was never touched on account of the complicated deadlocks on the doors and the electric alarm systems on every opening, even the air vents. In spite of it looking a bit like Fort Knox, it was really a very nice place.

It was filled with the usual crowd of refugees, kids who were too scared to go out into the playground in case Barry Hollis bashed them up. There were four monitors on duty at the desk, though one would have been plenty. All the library monitors at our school were a bit freaky, like Dennis Moyle who talked in a high little gossipy voice and hung round teachers asking if they needed any help or any messages run. You could always tell new teachers at our school. They were the ones still smiling at and still being polite to Dennis Moyle, but after a couple of weeks they found out what a crashing bore he was, though it took them the rest of the year to shake him off.

There was Margeart Collins who was so dim it took her a whole year to learn how to roll the library date stamp forward. Her name was really Margaret, but Margeart was how she always spelled it, even though she was in the sixth grade. There was Roa, who could hardly speak any English apart from the words Barry Hollis taught him on his first day at Barringa East Primary, and this weird hysterical girl named Leanne Jessop. Mrs Cheale, who was kind, felt sorry for them so let them all be library monitors.

They all turned and gawked at Alison when I introduced her to Mrs Cheale. 'You're the girl with the reading age of 14.6,' Mrs Cheale said, which just shows you how fast news travelled in our school. The system worked like this. The lady who ran the tuckshop came over to boil eggs in the staff room at 9.45 a.m. for egg and lettuce sandwich orders. While they were simmering she called in to Mrs Orlando's office to hear the latest gossip, and then she popped into all the classrooms to collect the lunch-baskets and pass the gossip on to the teachers.

Alison Ashley smiled modestly and told Mrs Cheale that she liked reading. Mrs Cheale took a real shine to her straight away. She showed Alison the new books that hadn't been processed yet. Usually if anyone dared lay a finger on any uncovered books, she changed from a patient teacher into a monster with fangs and a black velvet cloak.

She showed Alison all these books with gold medals on the covers that had won the Book of the Year awards, and Alison, naturally, had read every one of them, and was telling Mrs Cheale that her aunt was a librarian. Librarians always seem fascinated if you know someone else who is a librarian.

I suppose it's because they are cooped up with books all the time, and forget there are other librarians.

Mrs Cheale gave a little cry of delight, like a bird-watcher spotting a Red-kneed Dotterel in unfamiliar territory, and just ignored me standing there. I felt jealous and miffed. If there was one thing I couldn't stand, it was being ignored. I liked to have everyone's attention all the time, and anyhow, I was supposed to be the one showing Alison around the school. So I took the wooden tray of little cards away from Dennis Moyle and plonked it down in front of Alison. I started explaining with a great deal of authority, about the borrowing system. I thought Mrs Cheale might say, 'Erica is the most efficient person to show you how our library works, Alison. There's no person I rely upon more.' But what she said was, 'Yuk, will you kindly stop crashing around and raising your voice in this library? That notice on the door isn't there for decoration, you know.'

The notice said, 'Polite People Especially Welcome' and had been designed and constructed in the art and craft room. By me. I'd made all the letters look like vertical books, and it had taken a lot of time and creative energy, as well as a whole packet of felt pens.

I was extremely indignant that Mrs Cheale seemed to have forgotten that I had made that notice. I thought of just leaving those two chatting about books and libraries and the Dewey Decimal

System. I'd go and ask Mrs Orlando if I could have a soluble anti-irritant aspirin, though she said last year I would have to bring in a letter from my mother if I was going to be asking for strong medication every day.

But just then Mr Kennard led Barry Hollis in by the ear. Mr Kennard had found him in the playground defacing one of the library books with rude slogans. I would have liked to stay and watch Barry getting told off by Mrs Cheale, but Alison had already gone tactfully to the door and was waiting for me to show her some more things.

'Our library is architect designed,' I said ingratiatingly. (Although I was so jealous of her, at that stage I still wanted her to choose me for her best friend.)

'It's a nice little library,' she said. 'But at the school where I was last year, the library was about three times that size.'

I showed her where the toilets were, but she said she already knew because Mrs Orlando told her when she arrived that morning. I showed her where the bubblers were, and she said she usually didn't drink water from them because there was a danger of catching germs from kids putting their mouths right down on the spout. All the time while she was looking around inspecting everything, her smooth face didn't show any expression at all. I realized suddenly it was a mask. I knew that behind that mask she was thinking Barringa East Primary School was not much better than a council tip.

I showed her the sandpit and the little kids' part of the playground. I felt sorry for the prep-grade teacher, who never seemed to get any peace from her class. There was always some little kid with sand in its eyes bleating outside the staff room for Mrs Wentworth. So she usually took her lunch and cup of tea and her knitting and sat by the sandpit, even when it wasn't her turn for playground duty. She was so calm she didn't get excited, even when kids broke their collarbones. Mrs Wentworth would murmur, 'There's no need to cry, dear, we'll soon have it all better.' But first she would roll up her knitting and mark the place in her pattern book and put it back in her bag. She had four children of her own, but they didn't go to our school. (It was funny, but none of the teachers' kids was enrolled at our school. You'd have thought it would be more convenient for them.)

One of the little Tonkin kids came charging by, and I whispered to Alison, 'Don't get too close Those Tonkins always have nits, even though the nurse comes round and leaves free lotion. I've heard that lice can jump. Did you know that? They can jump from one kid's head to another kid's head.'

Now I personally thought that was a very interesting piece of medical information, but Alison Ashley went all peculiar. She turned pale under her tan and clamped both hands over her long swinging gold hair and kept them there.

'If you don't like looking at the little kids' playground, I'll show you the other things we have at this school,' I said. 'Except there's not all that much else. There's the tuckshop.'

'I always bring lunch from home,' Alison said.

'They have beaut iced donuts at the tuckshop.'

'I'm not allowed to eat junk food.'

'I can show you the sick bay,' I said.

'No, thanks,' said Alison. 'I don't like looking at grazed knees or anything like that. I don't like illness.'

Well! I knew then that it would be quite impossible for Alison Ashley and me ever to be best friends. I'd had a whole lot of various fascinating ailments ever since I was born in the back seat of Aunty Val's Mini. (Mum had left it too late to get to hospital, since she was in the middle of putting a henna rinse in her hair.) Best of all, I liked being sick enough to have antibiotic capsules with my name typed on the label by the chemist.

I looked at beautiful healthy Alison Ashley. She was staring around at Barringa East Primary with no expression at all on her soft pretty face. But I knew very well that inside her mind she was thinking that Barringa East Primary belonged to a late-night horror movie. And I got this tight feeling in my throat glands, like you do when you're coming down with a virus, only mine was caused by indignation.

Suddenly I thought of a whole lot of things we had going for us at Barringa East Primary. It wasn't fair that we were never mentioned in the local paper unless the school was burned down or busted into.

27

The nice things were ones the editor wouldn't think interesting enough for his rotten old paper. Such as Mr Nicholson, the Principal, who never acted stuck up just because he was a headmaster. If there was a dog fight going on in the playground, he always dived out and locked them up in the sports-equipment shed until the dog catcher's van arrived, so kids wouldn't get bitten. And what's more, he knew the name of every kid in the school. When he got out of his car in the morning he always said, 'Hi there, Marty, or Diane, or Greg (or whoever the kid was), how are things going?' And at Easter he always bought a bag of chocolate eggs and hid them around the sandpit for the preps to find.

And Mrs Cheale in the library who tried so hard to get kids taking books home even if they hardly ever did because they preferred watching *Prisoner* on TV.

And Miss Belmont who was a fantastic teacher even though she was so fierce.

And there was pale gold Alison Ashley looking down her nose at our school, and she hadn't even been there long enough to get clobbered by Barry Hollis!

'Well, Miss Belmont told me to show you round, and I have,' I said snakily. 'So now I can get back to my FRIENDS.'

I went into the sick bay and put pre-sterilized, waterproof band-aids on both of my elbows. There wasn't anything wrong with them, but band-aids always had a soothing effect on me.

28

FOUR

When school ended I hung round to spy on Alison
Ashley to see if she got collected. There was always
a line of mothers along the fence at 3.30. Alison was
waiting by the gate looking as though she'd just that
moment stepped out of a shower and got dressed in
fresh clothes, instead of putting in a day at school.
She was inspecting the Barringa East mums with
her innocent expression to which only I knew the
code.

None of the parents belonging to Barringa East
Primary School was what you could call a natty
dresser. Some of the mums had a cigarette dangling
from one hand and a toddler dangling from the
other, and some of them had their hair up in rollers.
And the waiting cars certainly were not anything
like the ones Princess Anne would have been collected in from school when she was a kid. There
were old Holden station wagons, or vans with a
firm's name printed on the side, or old bombs that
looked as though they wouldn't even have a

driveworthy certificate, let alone a roadworthy one.

Then someone turned up in a car for Alison Ashley. Glossy as a polished grapefruit, it just had to be her car. A lady reached over and opened the door and let old Alison in. Alison's mum. She looked exactly like Alison, only even more elegant. Her hair was wound around her head like a glamorous turban, and her hand resting on the door looked as though it had never dangled a toddler or a shopping basket in its life. Her expression was the same as Alison's, buttery smooth and showing no emotions or reactions or anything.

Alison got quickly into her golden coach as though she could hardly wait to get home and dive into a tub of disinfectant.

I dodged Jedda and went home by my private detour which she hadn't discovered yet. I wasn't going to walk through Barringa East with a little kid who whinnied and got down on her hands and knees to eat the grass on people's nature strips.

As I walked along thinking about Alison Ashley, my spirits sagged. I walked past the house where Miss Anastasia Wallace lived. She was out in her garden raving loudly to her plants. As usual, she was dressed in a tattered satin party dress, ankle socks, high-heeled shoes, and an old felt army hat with a bunch of poppies on the brim, only they looked more like bursting pomegranates. She was harmless, though she used to bail people up at the top of the escalator at the shopping centre and recite weird poetry to them. Only they never listened;

they sidled away quickly, looking very embarrassed.

Sometimes she looked up from her plants and said hello when you walked past her house. She never remembered anyone, and it was quite interesting waiting to see what she was going to call you. Sometimes when I said hello, she'd say, 'Oh, how are you today, Mrs Fawcett-Gibson?' or 'God bless you, Sister Veronica', or 'Hello, Jimmy, being a good boy?' But right then I looked glumly over the fence at poor crazy old Miss Anastasia Wallace and felt depressed. I couldn't be bothered calling out to her, but slunk past on tippy toes like a Hobyah.

I went by the Selly's house. Their front yard was filled with old prams and junk and cats, and they didn't even have newspaper over their front windows. You could look right in and see Mrs Selly breastfeeding her baby and yelling at all the other kids, the whole eight of them.

All the way down the street I kept noticing depressing things. There was a hideous birdbath in someone's front garden, made out of red concrete with a big green concrete frog on the rim. (It was so ugly that even the Eastside Boys left it alone, though Jedda liked it. She used to pretend it was a horse trough.)

No elegance anywhere. The street signs were bent at crazy angles from being swung on by the Eastside Boys, and the vandalized phone box outside the milkbar didn't just have its phone ripped out – there wasn't anything left of it except two walls. And every footpath had 'Eastside Boys Wuz Here' sprayed along it with aerosol spray paint.

I reached our house. Mum was not the sort of person any garden club would break their necks to get on their committee. (She liked plastic flowers because you never had to change the vase water, and they lasted longer.) Harley sometimes mowed the grass at the front of our place, usually when he'd spent his unemployment money and wanted to borrow some from mum. He never finished doing all the lawn at once; just enough to butter mum up. So our front yard was just an expanse of half-short, half-long grass and clover.

Mum's room was at the front of the house. She was mad about little ornaments and had them arranged along the window sill so passers-by could see them. Her ornaments were pink poodles with glitter collars, Spanish ladies, china kittens holding parasols, and pixies sitting on velvet mushrooms. I imagined I was Alison Ashley looking at them, and felt more depressed.

I went round the back of our place, climbing over Jedda's horse float which she made at the weekend on the back steps, just where people wanted to get in and out. It was made from a ladder, the wheelbarrow and the shower curtain, but Jedda was so spoiled that mum didn't even tell her off.

Mum was sitting at the kitchen table and Valjoy was giving her a manicure. You never saw so many bottles of nail varnish! The table looked as though it was a battlefield for hundreds of little white-helmeted marching soldiers, all wearing frosted plum, coral rose or pearl lustre tunics. Although Valjoy was taking a lot of care to give mum a really professional-looking manicure, they were fighting. They were always fighting about something.

Mum was really yelling. She was yelling, 'Valjoy, I'm sick of telling you off about those louts! You can say what you like, madam, but for sure that kid called Blonk or Spike or whatever nicked my gold-mesh sunglasses case last Saturday. He was the only one here in this kitchen except you. Charming, isn't it, when you can't leave a nice gold-mesh sunglasses case lying around in your own kitchen! Lennie gave me that last trip he made to Adelaide. It cost nearly $20. I went over to the chemist and priced it, and the only person could have nicked it apart from Blonk was you! Hullo, Erk love, how was school?'

Depressing.

She didn't even look up. She was watching Valjoy like an international chess champion to make sure she didn't use too much nail-bonding solution. Valjoy didn't look up, either, but she said, 'Listen, Erk, this is the last time I'm warning you to stay out of my room. Don't deny that you've been at my Charlie perfume, you creep. I made a secret mark on the bottle.'

Mum and Valjoy's perfume collection was nearly as large as their nail varnish one. I liked to wear perfume to school. It made me feel exotic.

I suddenly thought of Alison Ashley. She hadn't smelled of perfume. She had smelled of hair conditioner, apples, Pears soap, fresh Kleenex tissues, dry cleaning and new writing paper.

I opened the fridge to get a drink. Our fridge didn't look one bit elegant inside. It was crowded with left-over things on saucers, and tins of opened, Gladwrapped cat food. And frozen food such as pizzas, hamburgers, potato chips and Sara Lee cakes. Also a stockpile of Lennie's tinnies.

Alison Ashley's refrigerator would look straight out of a magazine advertisement, with beautiful desserts in parfait glasses, baked turkey garnished with parsley, jelly castles decorated with cream and mandarin slices, and jugs of freshly made orange juice with ice beads frosting the sides.

'THERE'S NEVER ANYTHING TO EAT OR DRINK IN THIS HOUSE EXCEPT JUNK FOOD!' I yelled furiously. (Sometimes after concussion you don't feel the reaction until hours later. And that was what was happening to me. I was suffering delayed culture shock from sitting next to Alison Ashley all day.)

I stood at the open fridge, like a primitive life form being engulfed in its ice-age breath. I looked with hatred at the packets of frozen ready-made donuts and frozen spaghetti bolognaise. A plastic bag tumbled out of the clutter and landed at my feet. It was full of grass clippings and had a label on it saying OTES. (Jedda was not very good at spelling.) I kicked the bag of otes across the floor and threw my school bag on top and jumped up and down on both and swore.

'That's lovely,' said Valjoy, as though she never ever said anything worse than 'Oh, dear' or 'Alas!'

'Erica!' yelled my mum. 'If my nails weren't still wet from this protein-reinforced base coat that cost $7.95, I'd get up and tan you! Next thing you'll have your little sister saying all those nasty words!'

'She never says anything except whinny and neigh,' I said bitterly. 'And I don't know why you're picking on me about swearing when you and Valjoy do it all the time.'

'Don't be cheeky.'

'And Lennie. You never say anything when he sits there swearing his head off, and that's just when he's making ordinary conversation. If you can call what he says conversation.'

'What do you mean?' Mum demanded. 'Lennie's very good company. You don't have to go to a university to get an education. Lennie's very brainy. He does all his own repairs and maintenance on his truck, and he's widely travelled. I won't have you making digs at Lennie behind his back, young lady, I'm warning you!'

'I'd certainly appreciate a warning if Lennie's coming to our place tonight,' I said. 'I'll go down the street and visit that crazy Miss Anastasia Wallace and get her to read some of her poetry. Even that'd be better than listening to boring old Lennie.'

Mum was very sensitive about Lennie, so she ordered me to go to my room and stay there, and good riddance. And that furthermore, I couldn't

35

have any frozen Bavarian cream cheesecake for dinner tonight, either.

I didn't care. I slammed the kitchen door so hard that the plastic tulips and plastic maidenhair fern on the hall table fell off. I stomped into my room and Jedda's, which was 90 per cent her room and the rest left over for me. I slammed that door, too, and then sat down and had a good cry in front of the mirror.

I always enjoyed having a good cry. The part of me that wanted to be an actress stood aside and looked on whilst I was bawling. I carefully studied the effect of my hooked hands clawing through my hair, and the best way to blink so that the tears rolled down evenly.

'It's not fair!' I sobbed into my hands. 'Life is full of injustice!' Then I thought of another good line, trying it out with different facial expressions. 'Just one more mile for to tote the weary load,' I said, and it sounded beautiful, though very sad and depressing. I cried some more, and wound it all up with a very powerful statement that always sounds exactly right when you want to end a crying session.

'I wish I were dead!' I said. I said it five times, each time stressing a different word and listening to the result, and then dried my eyes and felt a bit better. I looked round for something I could do to pay Jedda back for having to share a room with her. And for keeping me awake at nights making hoof noises in her sleep. She made them with the length of her tongue clamped up against her palate. (I investigated one night with a torch.)

She had about a thousand little plastic model horses all over her 90 per cent of the room, even on top of the wardrobe. I went around and laid each one on its back, so they looked as though they'd been stricken with a serious horse-disease.

Then I got out my magnifying mirror and had a good look at myself in the strong light. I wasn't pretty, but actresses shouldn't be, anyhow. What they really need are dynamic and compelling looks. I felt that I had dynamic and compelling cheek-bones, and also a warm, generous mouth. (Though Valjoy said it was just plain big.)

But while I was examining my face in the mirror, I kept thinking of Alison Ashley. Suddenly I craved to look like her, and talk like her and have a mother and a car like hers, and the same clothes and pretty manners, and that she would let me be her best friend. Even if I hated her. I thought gloomily that Alison Ashley most likely never in her life was sent to her room for swearing. Probably she didn't even know any bad words, though going to Barringa East would soon fix that. And if she ever did get sent to her room, she would probably sit down and clean her nails which never got dirty anyhow, or use the time to revise her tables which she already knew off by heart. Or tidy all her socks into paired rolls. And furthermore, I bet that every six months when she went to the dentist, she never had cavities.

Life was full of injustice.

FIVE

Next day at school Miss Belmont handed back our projects. At the start of the term, our school had gone to see a ballet, *Peter and the Wolf*. It was supposed to be a back-to-school treat, but Miss Belmont made our grade do an assignment on it. I hadn't minded. She had mine at the bottom of the pile on the desk. It was about ten times as thick as anyone else's. I'd got a bit carried away.

Before she handed them back she told off the whole grade for being time wasting and lazy (all except Alison Ashley, who hadn't started at our school when the assignment was given out. And me.). 'Erica Yurken's was the only project worth looking at,' Miss Belmont scolded. 'As for this disgraceful effort of yours, Barry Hollis, words fail me!'

Barry Hollis's project, written on the back of an old envelope, had only two sentences saying, 'I never been to a theaer in my hole life and I dont wantto', and 'If I knew any guy lerning ballay I

38

would bash him.' Miss Belmont was waving it around angrily while she was telling Barry off and I saw Alison Ashley lean forward to read the two sentences, but she didn't look shocked or anything. Maybe she was getting used to sixth-grade life at Barringa East Primary.

Shane Corbet's assignment had a heading, 'The Killer Instinct in Wolf Packs', and a biro picture of a pack of wolves dragging some startled-looking Russian peasants off a sleigh. It didn't contain one word about ballet. Miss Belmont made him tear it up and put it in the bin with Barry's. By the time she reached the bottom of the pile of assignments, the bin was choked with torn-up paper. Then she picked mine up.

One agreeable thing about school was when you had a chance to make everyone else in the grade look dumb. For my project, I'd borrowed some of the silky paper Mrs Orlando used for the spirit copying machine, and also a new manila folder. I had drawn a picture of two theatre masks on the cover, with a border of ballerinas. I put on an expression of dignified modesty while Miss Belmont was showing my project to the class and saying how well presented it was and why couldn't they do the same. I even stopped minding so much that Alison Ashley wore a new outfit; beautiful white jeans, pale-blue broderie anglaise blouse, tiny pearl-stud earrings, and her hair brushed back and caught up in a pearl clasp.

'Take your project down to the office, Erica,'

Miss Belmont said. 'It might be a consolation for Mr Nicholson to find that SOME people in this grade are capable of work.'

Mr Nicholson was very impressed with my assignment and asked if he could borrow it for display purposes when the inspector came around. He really liked it, I could tell, so I spread my assignment out on his desk and started at the front, turning the pages over very slowly so he wouldn't miss out on anything. I showed him the places where Miss Belmont had written excellent, and the centre-piece I painted of red-velvet curtains with gold tassels. I read aloud the text on each page in case he had difficulty with my writing. But I was hardly three-quarters of the way through when he remembered that he had some important telephone calls to make, and said that he'd look at my project some other time when he had more chance to do it justice.

Then I showed it to Mrs Orlando, but she didn't really appreciate culture, even though she was a highly trained secretary who could do Pitman's shorthand. She went on typing maths stencils like a runaway steam train, and just glanced up and said, 'Yes, Yuk, very nice.'

So I took it along to the library and showed Mrs Cheale, and then as I thought it was a shame the other teachers didn't have a chance to see it, too, I called in to every class room. Also the tuckshop to show the mothers on duty there. On the way back I dropped in to the sick bay and checked the contents of the first-aid box which was used on excursions. I made a list of supplies that were running low, and also put down some new medicines which I'd seen advertised on television. Mrs Orlando wasn't terribly grateful when I gave the list to her. 'Aren't you supposed to be in art and craft right now?' she demanded.

Our art and craft teacher, Miss Lattimore, really did her best to make our art classes interesting, even though having a kid like Barry Hollis in a room along with jars of poster paint and wet clay must have been like teaching next to a ticking bomb.

Our art classes had been even more interesting since we got the dark-room and could learn about photography. Only Barry Hollis wasn't allowed to set foot in the dark-room anymore, because once he'd fixed the electric timer so that it buzzed non stop and couldn't be turned off.

We took photographs with the school camera whenever we went on school excursions, and Miss Lattimore always managed to get one of Barry Hollis sitting somewhere in disgrace. On every excursion, he did something to give our school a bad name. Or a worse one, Miss Lattimore said, than the one it had already. There was a whole stack of Barry Hollis-in-exile pictures – one of him the time he got sprung opening the emergency exit in the bus instead of using the steps like everyone else. And one of him getting yelled at by a man at the Victoria Market for pulling a coconut from the bottom row of a display. And pictures of him getting told off by officials at National Trust houses, security

41

guards at Tullamarine Airport, VicRail guards, and a very cross lady in a sari at the Handcrafts of India fair.

As there was an interschool student photography competition coming up, Miss Lattimore said each of us could take a photo of something suitable in the playground.

'I'll show Alison Ashley, the new girl, how to work the camera,' I said. I really enjoyed showing people new things. It was a very satisfying feeling if they didn't catch on to instructions right away, and you could say, 'There's not much point in showing you. I'm sorry, but certain things are just beyond the scope of some people.'

But Alison put up her hand. She always put up her hand before she talked in class, and in Barringa East Primary it looked peculiar, this solitary, straight-as-a-flagpole hand up in the air, when everyone else was just calling out. Miss Lattimore nodded approvingly at her, and Alison said she already knew how to work an Olympus Trip camera, also a movie camera, and she'd already had some dark-room lessons at her last school. She didn't sound as though she was actually showing off. She was pleasant and polite as always, but I felt extremely irritated. Up to then I'd been the only student at Barringa East who knew that the red light over the dark-room door wasn't there just to teach the prep kids traffic drill.

'Well then, having someone with experience will make our photography programme more interesting,' said Miss Lattimore. 'Especially for the members of this class who already think they know it all and can't be taught any more by anyone.' (Naturally she meant Barry Hollis, although she was looking in my direction. Perhaps the look was meant to include approval of me as well as Alison Ashley, as I helped supervise the school photography programme. I often turned up early and changed the corridor displays without waiting to be asked, to save Miss Lattimore the bother of doing it herself.)

Out in the playground, Barry Hollis suggested photographing the girls coming out of the boys' toilets and the boys coming out of the girls' toilets, but Miss Lattimore just looked at him witheringly. Margeart Collins had the first dithery turn with the camera. She tried to take a picture of a sparrow, but it flew off before she even worked out where the viewfinder was. 'Never mind, Margaret,' said Miss Lattimore. 'Maybe it will turn out to be a very nice picture of Twisty crumbs on asphalt.'

Kevin Cossan took a corny shot of Lisa making out she was shooting a netball goal. The next six people had similar tired ideas. No one else in our grade except me had any imagination whatever. Then it was Alison's turn with the camera.

She had her picture all worked out. She squinted through the viewfinder judging angles, only of course Alison Ashley didn't really squint, she just peeped prettily. She climbed up the ladder of the suspended tunnel bridge made of old car tyres, and took a slow, careful photograph. Everyone jeered about how dumb it was, photographing a lot of old tyres. But I looked over her shoulder and saw that the tyres curved into a wonderful pattern of light and shade. I wished jealously that I had thought of it first.

'That's very good, Alison,' Miss Lattimore said. 'It's nice to find someone who can keep her eyes open and find something out of the ordinary.' Alison wound on the film and handed me the camera.

I went twice round the oval peeping prettily at various things through the viewfinder, and came back. 'About time, too!' kids snarled impatiently. 'Come on, Yuk, hand it over.'

'I haven't taken my picture yet,' I said.

'Honestly,' said Miss Lattimore. 'You are . . .'

'But I've thought of something very artistic,' I said. 'I'm going to take a close-up picture of bark.'

The immature people in our grade sat up and dangled their paws and yapped. 'Stop that silly yelping,' Miss Lattimore said angrily. 'And Barry Hollis, you stupid boy, untie Margaret from that goal post at once. I've told you before not to take macrame string from the craft room.'

I went hunting for a tree with suitable artistic bark. It took a long time. There weren't many trees in our playground on account of the Eastside Boys ripping up shrubs as quickly as the parents' club put them in. But there was one eucalyptus tree near the fence. I enjoyed taking photographs; a camera always made me feel like a newspaper reporter, as though I had done a lot of slick dangerous living and worked in a skyscraper. I took pictures of the tree from every possible angle, and somehow used up all the film in the camera.

I didn't really mean to, but Miss Lattimore turned very snitchy when she saw that the dial was at thirty-six. Everyone carried on about missing out, although it would have been a waste of good film, anyhow, letting them have a try. Their idea of taking pictures was to snap each other pulling down the red part of their eyelids.

'Next art session the people with worthwhile negatives can prepare a really good print for the competition,' Miss Lattimore said when she was through telling me off. 'Barry Hollis, get off that rubbish-bin lid at once and let that person out. Don't be so unhygienic.'

We went back to our room for lunch and Alison got out her smart white lunchbox. This time she had a wholemeal salad roll practically hopping out of its compartment with vitamins, an apple polished like a Christmas-tree ornament, a health bar made out of sesame seeds, wheatgerm and honey, and a drink bottle filled with tomato juice.

My lunch was weird, as it usually was on the days I brought it from home instead of buying it. I hadn't been able to find any lunchwraps, so I'd put it all into a used waxed cornflakes bag. I had a thawed-out, pre-cooked frozen rissole, an Irish stew sandwich, and a grotty looking pear, which looked dead on the outside, but was okay in the middle. Some cornflakes were stuck to its skin. I saw Alison Ashley look at it in disbelief and flinch.

Miss Belmont was putting notices up in the corridor, so it was possible to talk. 'Are you going to the high school or the tech next year, Alison?' I asked out of curiosity. Our local high school had even a worse name than Barringa East Primary. Everyone said they flushed the heads of new kids in the toilets as a welcoming ceremony on their first day. The tech was where my sister Valjoy went. They'd turned it into a co-ed school two years ago, and still had only a small enrolment of girls, which was why Valjoy chose it instead of the high school. Parents were a bit nervous about sending their girls to the tech, as it had even a worse name than Barringa East Primary and the high school put together. But Valjoy enjoyed being the only female in the metal-welding class. She liked being outnumbered by a vast horde of wild and daring boys.

'I won't be going to either,' Alison said. 'My mother put my name down for Kyle Grammar School. She tried to get them to take me earlier, when we found out about the new school zoning. But they didn't have a vacancy till next year.'

A bit of cold Irish stew sandwich stuck in my throat. You could see Kyle Girls Grammar School from the train going into town. It was just like a school out of an English story book. The girls there wore beautiful pale-blue uniforms with little navy-blue bowler hats and gloves, and if they travelled on the train they always stood up for adults. Once when I was in the same carriage with a couple of them, they found this paper bag with a bottle of expensive skin-moisturizing lotion on the seat, and they handed it in to the station attendant. I was so impressed by such honesty that I told Valjoy when I got home. But she went straight up to the station and asked if anyone had handed in a bottle of skin moisturizer because she'd bought some for her Gran's birthday and left it in a carriage, and they gave it to her.

Every time I looked out of the train and saw Kyle Grammar School I ached with jealousy. I would have adored to go to a school like that, and wear a Latin motto on my blazer pocket. And end up as a prefect, or better still, the head girl. At Barringa High School they'd given up trying to make the kids wear uniforms years ago, and I didn't think they'd ever had prefects, because the kids there didn't take notice of the teachers, let alone other kids. I was sure I'd fit into a school like Kyle without any difficulty at all. It wasn't fair that I'd never be able to go there. Alison Ashley already had everything, and Kyle Girls Grammar School, too, to look forward to next year.

'Oh, that place,' I said airily. 'They don't teach you anything there except how to cook for dinner parties and play tennis. I'll be going to Barringa High. From choice. They've got a new science block, and a choice of five languages, and for sport they do scuba diving, and they have sit-in strikes and mass demonstrations and lots of other interesting things.'

So there, Alison Ashley, I thought. Swallow that along with your old vitamins.

'You're wrong about Kyle,' Alison said. 'It had the highest HSC results of any school in the state last year.'

So there, Erica Yurken, her blue eyes said. Eat that along with your disgusting old pear, you mouldy peasant.

'Barringa High School has a computer room,' I said. 'And it also has a drama course. They give a big concert every year, and last year they did *Arsenic and Old Lace*.' I didn't tell her that the performance was cancelled because the Eastside Boys broke into the assembly hall beforehand and did something peculiar to the lighting.

'Well, at Kyle you can study ballet,' she said. 'Oh, I meant to tell you. You made the shoes look funny, on those ballet girls you drew for your assignment. They don't have a whole lot of criss-crosses. Ballet-shoe ribbons just cross over once and wrap around the ankle.'

'Not always,' I said, 'I went to a ballet last year, a proper one, not just *Peter and the Wolf*. It was a famous Russian ballet company doing *Swan Lake*, and they had their ribbons crossing over and over right up to their knees. Pale blue ribbons to match their dresses.'

Alison didn't say anything in her usual annoying way, but she raised her eyebrows.

'I went backstage after the performance,' I said. 'I know a lot of people in the theatre. And I was allowed to help those ballerinas take off their ballet slippers and pack them away ready to go back to Russia.'

'It must have been a very peculiar *Swan Lake*,' said Alison. 'They always wear white in *Swan Lake*. As far as I know swans aren't ever blue. And they certainly wouldn't have had their ballet slipper ribbons going right up to their knees.'

I bit savagely into my pear, which collapsed messily. I didn't have anything to clean it off the desk with except my half-eaten Irish stew sandwich. 'You just think you're great, Alison Ashley!' I said, exploding like my pear. 'You think you know everything! You think you're great just because you live over on Hedge End Road!'

'I've got to live somewhere, haven't I?' she said snappily. 'And do you mind wiping your lunch off my folder cover, if it's not too much trouble?'

Dianne and Leanne and Bev and everyone looked at us with interest. You can't mistake a fight shaping up promisingly in a class room.

'You think you're so fantastic!' I said. 'You look down your nose at everyone and everything in this school! You snob!'

'Good on yer, Yuk,' said Barry Hollis.

'You mind your own business, Barry Hollis, and

stay out of private conversations,' I said coldly.

'I am not a snob!' Alison said. 'What about you, anyhow, showing off all the time! You've done nothing except show off ever since I came to this school!'

'Yeah,' said Barry Hollis. 'Good on yer, Alison Ashley!'

'You mind your own business and keep out of private conversations,' Alison said, and her voice wasn't polite and quiet anymore, it was all over the place and high up, like mine.

Miss Belmont came in and stared at us. Alison busily fitted the lids on her lunchbox and drink bottle. I dumped my pear-flavoured Irish stew wet-tex into the waxed cornflake bag, and twisted it up viciously.

'Grade six, you may go out to play, now,' Miss Belmont said.

I went along to the sick bay instead and asked Mrs Orlando if I could have some of the new brand of ear drops and an antacid tablet. She told me to put a bit of cottonwool in my ear if it was hurting, and not to gobble my lunch and I wouldn't get indigestion. 'Go outside and play in the fresh air, Yuk,' she said, not even looking up from her Gestetner machine.

Mrs Orlando was a lousy sick-bay attendant.

SIX

We didn't speak to each other for a whole week.

Every day she wore something new to school and every day her work folder collected A's and flattering comments from Miss Belmont. All the teachers doted on her in a very sickening manner. At assembly they'd be hectoring their classes into what passed for straight lines at Barringa East Primary, and they'd turn and look at Alison Ashley standing there as polite and nicely brought up as a nativity angel, and their eyes would glimmer with faint hope for the human race. Maybe they thought Alison's excellent qualities would spread around the whole school and infect everyone, like gastro-enteritis.

But it was peculiar, because none of the other kids took to her at all. She was just so private and never started conversations or yakked on about herself. So everyone sort of skated warily around her, not stirring her, because kids who were that pretty and that well dressed didn't get stirred. But they acted as though she didn't really belong to our school at all, as though she was just a visitor.

The same way they treated me.

The tension between Alison Ashley and myself caused us to sit as far apart as possible from each other in class. If her work slid over to my side of the desk, I shoved it right back, and if any of my lunch crumbs got over on her side, she'd shovel them back with her ruler, as though they'd been sprayed with poisonous toxins.

With this cold war going on between us, you wouldn't have supposed for one minute that she'd turn up uninvited at my house and get herself asked for tea.

This was how it happened.

It was late Friday afternoon. Lennie was at the kitchen table, back from Wollongong, or wherever he'd been with his old truck, and he was not only sitting at our table, but mum was sitting on his knee. I found that extremely embarrassing. She was much too old in my opinion to have a boyfriend, anyhow. Not that Lennie was my idea of anyone's boyfriend, with his bald patch and his feeble jokes that were about a million years old. (Such as if Valjoy asked mum for money for the pictures and mum said, 'Try and get in for half, love', Lennie would be bound to say, 'Which half of you wants to go?')

'I thought I told you not to wear my silver slave bangles to school?' Valjoy said when I came in. (Every time Valjoy and I met, she began conversations with that phrase: I thought I told you.)

'Erk can be my slave girl any old tick of the

clock,' said Lennie. 'Come on, Erk, do us a belly dance. What's the good of wanting to go on the stage if you can't do a spot of belly dancing?' (That shows you the level of his conversation.)

'We're having a barbecue tonight, Erk,' mum said. 'And Len's shouting us to the drive-in after.'

'Are we supposed to be going in Lennie's truck? If so, I'm not coming. What if I saw anyone I knew there?'

'So what if you did?' demanded mum. 'Honest, Erk, you're getting that sour and critical lately. You never have a nice word to say to anyone in this house. It'll do you good, madam, starting at Barringa High next year and have your head flushed in the toilet.'

'That's a complete myth,' I said. 'Anyhow, I'd kill anyone who tried to flush my head in a toilet.'

'That's the goods,' Lennie said. 'I like a slave girl with a bit of spirit.'

I didn't answer him, because if there was one thing Lennie didn't need, it was encouragement. I cleared a space on the kitchen table to mix up some lemon cordial. This is what I had to clear away: a library book about astral projection; a pair of fake eyelashes; three empty beer cans; a black lace bra; a million horse swapcards; the *Turf Guide*; a plastic tub of shop-made potato salad that had been left out of the fridge and now sprouted a topping of penicillin; a bottle of shoe dye; and the cat. Our cat was a black tom called Norm with a horrible nature, and he swivelled around and bit me on the wrist.

There wasn't a scrap of gracious living at our house.

The doorbell rang. I didn't bother to get up and answer it, because the last four times when I did, it was to see the back view of Barry Hollis nicking off down the street.

'I'll get it,' said Valjoy. 'I'm expecting Spider and Blonk and Poison. We're going round to Macker's house to see his Suzuki.'

'If Spider's the one with the head like a hard-boiled egg sliced off at the top, and the python tattoo, and the safety pin through his ear, I don't want you asking him in, Valjoy,' mum said strictly. 'Last time he was here, he washed his leather jacket in the sink without even asking first.'

I sipped moodily at my lemon cordial through a straw. At least using a straw can give you a feeling of refined living, although it can't be compared to drinking champagne out of a crystal glass with a stem.

Valjoy yelled from the hall, 'Mum, tell Blonk and Poison when they come that we've gone round to Macker's anyway. And Erk, here's a kid from your school wants to see you, can't think why.'

I looked up, and there was Alison Ashley in our kitchen.

I would, from humiliation, have trickled down under the table and stayed there for ever, but the area under our table was pretty crowded. As well as people's legs, there was this huge stockpile of ironing, and the vacuum cleaner, and a half-built stable complex belonging to Jedda.

'Hullo, love,' said mum to Alison Ashley. 'You in the same class as Erk?'

'I took home Erica's pencil case by mistake, Mrs Yurken,' Alison said, so politely. 'I thought I'd better return it because of all the homework we've got to do over the weekend. I'm sorry, I guess I must have picked it up accidentally with my things.' She put my pencil case down on the table next to Valjoy's black lace bra and the false eyelashes.

My pencil case wasn't a proper one. It was just a cardboard box decorated with ballerina pictures, drawn by me. I noticed with mortification that I'd drawn all the ballet shoes with dozens of straps crossing over and over.

'Hey, sweetheart, you're a good looker,' Lennie said to Alison. 'Reckon I'll go back to school. Fillies didn't look like you when I was at school.'

(I personally didn't believe that Lennie ever went to school at all. I think he just groped his way out of a forest covered in bark and lichen like something out of a science-fiction story.)

'Say thank you about the pencil case, Erk,' mum said. 'Where's your manners?'

'Thanks,' I muttered into my lemon-flavoured junk food.

'Tell you what, love,' mum said to Alison. 'We're having a barbecue. So why don't you stay and have tea with us?'

I prayed for Lennie to swallow the flip top off his beer can and have to be rushed to hospital. I concentrated on sending mum ESP messages all screaming out NO! But my mum was abnormally sociable, and you could tell she was thrilled to bits that finally some kid from school was dropping in at our house.

I hurled ESP messages at Alison Ashley screaming, 'Don't you dare stay here! I don't want you! Get back to Hedge End Road where you belong!'

But all Alison said was, 'Thank you very much for the invitation, Mrs Yurken. There's no need to ring my mother. She'll be working late tonight, so I was home by myself anyhow. I'm sure she wouldn't mind if I stayed, as long as I get home before dark.'

I could have died.

'You and Erk might want to play records in her room till tea's ready,' said mum. 'Erk's just mad about that group Splunge, or Splurge or whatever they're called. She's got their album. Plays it non-stop.'

I really could have died.

Splurge was a group all the little kids in grade five and younger raved about, and I certainly didn't wish to advertise to Alison Ashley of all people that I owned their album. I dragged myself numbly up the hall, with her following, and hesitated at the door of my bedroom. I thought of the horrific mess Jedda's side was in. She'd set up some carton steeple chase hurdles down the middle of the room, and her mattress and bedding were rolled up on the floor. I kept telling her that she'd grow up all twisted like an espalier fruit tree if she slept there, but she never took any notice of me, maybe because I didn't look like a racehorse trainer.

I couldn't invite Alison Ashley into that weird-looking room. So I opened the door of Valjoy's and said, 'This is my room.'

Valjoy had a weekend job at the milkbar, and she spent all the money left over from buying clothes on interior decorating. She'd painted the walls black and the ceiling gold, and a huge stereo, which Blonk gave her for her fifteenth birthday, took up almost one wall. Mum wasn't too happy about having it in the house, because she said Blonk certainly couldn't have afforded such an expensive set by legal means. Sometimes when the police sirens were wailing up and down Wilga Street late at night after the East-side Boys, mum became nervous enough to unscrew the handle off Valjoy's bedroom door, so if the police accused her of harbouring stolen property, they couldn't get at the evidence in a hurry.

Valjoy had a fake leopard-fur bedspread, a pink plush elephant the size of Lennie, and a yellow bean bag. I sprawled casually on the leopard-skin bedspread. 'You can look through my record collection if you like,' I said. 'That's not really true, what mum said about me liking Splurge. You know how parents get things wrong. My little sister is the one who's rapt in Splurge.'

Alison inspected Valjoy's vast collection of

albums. Valjoy used to go with this boy who worked in a record shop, and he was always giving her records which he got at a discount. Or more likely pinched.

'It's a pity, but I can't play any for you right now,' I said, 'The stereo needs a new needle. I'm terribly fussy about scratching my records.' The truth was that I didn't know how to work Valjoy's record player, which had as many dials and knobs as an intensive-care unit. Also, she'd said she'd paralyse me if she caught me anywhere near it. 'You can look at my clothes if you want to,' I said. 'Just slide open the wardrobe doors.'

Alison didn't say anything, but she riffled along the long line of coathangers. Valjoy had thirteen pairs of jeans and twice that many tops, and a pair of shiny fake-leather pants, and a lot of dresses mum wouldn't let her wear in public unless she put a cardigan on over the top.

'Are you allowed to wear high heels?' Alison asked.

Valjoy had all these pairs of strappy shoes with heels as high as lighthouses. 'Of course I'm allowed to,' I said.

'How come you never wear any of these clothes to school?' Alison asked.

'I save them for the Cascade Disco on Saturday nights.'

'Are you really allowed to go to that place?'

'That's what I use all that make up for,' I said, waving airily at Valjoy's dressing table. Valjoy knew a boy whose mother was an Avon lady, and she was always receiving gifts of cosmetics, though mum said that boy's mother must wonder why her stocks were always running low.

'You can try on any of that make up,' I said. 'I've got plenty. Help yourself to some of that blue eyeshadow with the glittery stuff in it.'

'I don't think I'd better,' said Alison Ashley. 'I'm not allowed to wear make up. My mother would be cross.'

My mother would be cross! Honestly! Everyone else I knew would say 'Mum would chuck a mental' or 'I'd get a clip over the ear.'

Alison sat down in the bean bag. I'd always thought that there was no possible way anyone, even the Queen, could plonk down into a beanbag and still look dignified. But Alison Ashley managed to. One minute she was standing up looking at Valjoy's warpaint, and the next she was sitting gracefully in that beanbag with her ankles crossed and her hands folded neatly in her lap.

I picked up one of Valjoy's glossy magazines and flipped through the pages. When I came to the centrefold I was embarrassed and quickly put the magazine back.

'I guess you've done all that homework already?' I said crossly.

'I haven't even thought about the homework yet,' Alison said. 'I'm not all that interested in homework. I did marsupials in grade four, anyhow.'

'Miss Belmont is a fantastic teacher.'

'I never said she wasn't.'

'Everyone does their homework in her class. Even Barry Hollis always turns in something, even if it's just a couple of sentences. We're lucky to have her for our grade teacher.'

Alison Ashley didn't say anything for a long time. Vanquished.

'Was that your dad out there in the kitchen?' she asked, changing the subject.

'Certainly not!' I said indignantly. I considered various ways I could explain Lennie. I could say mum was a psychiatrist and Lennie one of her patients. Or that he was our gardener, only that would have sounded peculiar because our front yard was so primitive.

'I thought he must be your dad because your mother was sitting on his knee,' Alison said.

Could I say Lennie was my grandfather? She'd never believe that, because he didn't look quite that old enough, and ladies my mum's age probably didn't go round sitting on their father's knee, anyhow.

'He's a friend of hers,' I said sulkily. 'But she doesn't really like him. He's not her boyfriend or anything like that. Her real boyfriend's fantastic. He's very handsome and he owns a racehorse stud-farm and a Mercedes. He's going to buy mum a fur coat the day she agrees to marry him. I help train the racehorses at that place he has.'

'Really?'

'I just said so, didn't I? My real father is dead.'

'Oh,' said Alison. 'Sorry.'

My real dad wasn't dead at all. Last thing we heard was that he was wanted in Queensland for selling shares in a non-existent tin mine.

'My father was killed in a plane crash,' I said. 'He was a test pilot. When he knew the plane was going to crash, he flew out over the ocean and crashed there so he wouldn't come down on any houses. Every year on the anniversary of his death, I take a big wreath of roses down to the beach and cast it out to the tide. But you'd better not mention to my mum that I told you about my father getting killed. She never got over it.'

'But I thought you said she had a boyfriend with a racehorse stud-farm now?'

'What's that got to do with it?' I demanded. 'My mum's very popular. She's a hotel manageress. They have big wedding receptions there. When they get really busy, I help out. I wear a black dress and black high heels and a little white frilly apron and serve pre-dinner drinks to the customers.'

'Oh,' said Alison Ashley.

Her face never seemed to reflect moods at all like normal faces. You just couldn't tell what she was thinking deep down in those Royal Show Blue Ribbon eyes. She made me feel nervous, and when I felt nervous I always talked a lot to cover up.

'We're only living in Barringa East because my brother is training to be a missionary,' I said. 'He works amongst socially disadvantaged people. He's a monk, only while he's away from his monastery, he doesn't wear that brown dressing-gown thing that monks on TV usually do. He has special permission to wear jeans. Only you mustn't tell anyone I told you about Harley, because they have to take a vow of secrecy, all those monks.'

'Oh,' said Alison Ashley.

'So we're only renting this house until Harley finishes his missionary training,' I said. 'Our real house is in that suburb where Kyle Grammar School is. That's where we really live. But it's all shut up now, with a cover over the heated inground swimming pool. Lennie, the man you saw out in the kitchen, he's a private security guard. He just came over here to tell mum he checked up on our other house to see no one's broken into it while we're living in Barringa East so Harley can dedicate his life to the poor.'

'Erk!' yelled Jedda. 'Mum says the barbecue's ready and you and that other girl got to come out now.'

She banged open the door of Valjoy's room and glanced at Alison, only without much interest because Alison had Roman sandals on instead of hooves. 'What are you doing in Valjoy's . . .' she began, but I shot up and pushed her out into the hall. 'Come and see my new stable bed I made,' she said, grabbing Alison's hand. 'You can crawl in and have a sleep if you like.'

I hastily snatched Alison's other hand and tugged her towards the kitchen. It was like one of those scenes where they tie a victim to four wild horses to get the truth out of them, only I think Alison would have managed to look poised and graceful even if that was happening to her.

But Jedda shoved open the door of our room, and I could have died. There was the usual revolting sight of all her weekly snacks on the floor next to the hooped-up mattress. And since she wasn't using her bed to sleep in, she'd dumped every single toy and article of clothing she owned on the wire base. She said it was quicker than hunting for things through the chest of drawers. Disorder, chaos, shame and utter mortification.

Alison Ashley looked at Jedda's part of the room and blinked incredulously. Then she glanced at my bed. There was the red tracksuit top I wore to school most days slung over one bed post, and my school bag over the other. And my Barringa East Primary School gym skirt and top lying on the spread. Also my Splurge album with my name on it in big purple texta letters.

'I sleep in this room sometimes because Jedda gets bad dreams,' I said. 'When she was a baby she was trapped in a burning pram for several hours before being rescued.'

'Was I?' asked Jedda with interest.

'Tea, I mean dinner, is ready,' I said quickly.

The barbecue was really terrible. I died every few minutes. It seemed to me that every person in our family was trying their hardest to act and sound and look like people who lived in caves, to show me up in front of Alison Ashley.

Jedda handed her a sausage. Just a sausage by itself, with no plate or fork or anything, and Alison looked at it and said politely, 'Could I have a paper tissue, please?'

Lennie shook up a can of Coke and squirted mum with it, and she squirted him back with the hose. Our cat jumped up on the barbecue (he wasn't scared of anything, even fire), grabbed a steak and snarled and flexed his claws when Lennie tried to make him give it back. Mum yelled out to Harley that the food was getting cold, and he strolled out of his bungalow wearing underpants which had a pattern of red ants on a black background. I thought gloomily that even Alison Ashley wouldn't believe that any monastery would let him wear clothes like that.

'Harley,' scolded mum. 'Get back in there and put some jeans or a towel on! You'll embarrass Alison. Have you got any pain-in-the-neck brothers, love?'

'No, there's only me,' said Alison. 'I'm the only child.'

I just knew it. I would have adored being somebody's only child. The centre of everything, with a pile of presents every Christmas and birthday, and a bedroom all to myself with a canopied four-poster bed and an *en suite*.

'Have some sauce,' I said sourly.

Our awful barbecue went on and on. Valjoy came home with Blonk, Spider, Ace and Titch. Alison Ashley looked at them expressionlessly, but tucked her clean little sandals in under the garden bench. She still held the sausage daintily in one hand but she'd hardly eaten any of it.

Spider and Blonk revved up an argument about motor-bike rally tickets and three dollars missing change. Mum raised her voice over theirs and told them to shut up and stop that punching and bad language and nick off to their own house if they had one, which she doubted. They wouldn't do either, so Lennie grabbed Spider by the collar of his leather jacket, and Blonk by the seat of his jeans, and lugged them round to the front and dumped them over the fence.

'It's not fair!' cried Valjoy. 'I'm never allowed to bring my friends home!'

'Don't give me that!' Mum yelled back. 'This place is always neck deep in creepy-looking tech kids who've been suspended from school.'

Valjoy could never stand her friends being criticized, so another battle started and hamburger buns were thrown. Alison's expression didn't change one bit. After a while she got up and said she'd better get home before dark. She thanked mum politely for asking her to stay for dinner and said she'd had a very nice time – the liar.

She said goodbye to Jedda, Harley, Lennie, Ace, Titch, and even Valjoy, who was sulking by herself under the clothes line because mum had won the fight. Mum had a louder and bossier voice than Valjoy.

'You're a real nice well-behaved kid, Alison,'

mum said. 'You come round any time you like and play with Erk. I'm glad she's found you for a girlfriend at school. She doesn't get along very well with other kids as a rule. Erk, where are your manners? Get up off your numberplate and show your girlfriend to the gate and say tata nicely.'

Miss Anastasia Wallace was stalking along the footpath in her high-heeled shoes and ankle socks, with an empty supermarket bag over her arm. She was looking furtively over everyone's fences. As well as reciting her weird poetry in public, she went around Barringa East pinching people's cats.

'You can get back to Hedge End Road if you cut across the oval,' I said distantly to Alison Ashley. 'Only watch out for Barry Hollis. He always bashes kids up if they go across the oval.'

'Does he?' Alison asked in surprise. 'That's funny. He was really nice when I met him on the way over. I asked him where your house was, and he even walked a bit of the way to show me.'

'Barry Hollis always bashes kids up,' I said. 'He can't help it. It's like a nervous twitch.'

'He asked me to come and watch him play football when the season starts,' Alison said, as smug as a Porsche owner.

Miss Anastasia Wallace passed our gate. She turned around and to me she said, 'Hello, Brian. Thank you for unblocking that gully trap, you're a kind, thoughtful boy.' And to Alison Ashley she said, 'Mrs Jagger, you can deny it all you like, but that brown tabby you claim you've had for six months is my Clarissa who went missing three weeks ago. I shan't put up with it. If you don't return her, I'll be forced to notify the police. Good afternoon.'

Alison stared after her.

'Don't take any notice,' I said bitterly. 'She's just a neighbour. All our neighbours are like that, one way or another.'

'It's certainly very different from Hedge End Road,' said Alison Ashley.

Well then, Valjoy and mum weren't the only ones in my family who could yell. 'Of all the nerve, Alison Ashley!' I yelled. 'How dare you criticize Barringa East and stare at poor dotty old Miss Anastasia as though she's crazy or something! I never even invited you around here in the first place!'

'What are you yelling at me for?' Alison said. 'What on earth did I do, Yuk?'

'Don't you call me Yuk! And my pencil case never did get caught up with your things. I remember putting it right down the bottom of my school bag. You just took it for an excuse to come round here and stickybeak. You are the most low-down person I ever met in my life, Alison Ashley, and get back to Hedge End Road, which is probably just as redundant and boring as you are. And I personally wouldn't ever dream of stickybeaking at your house, because you and it hold no interest for me at all. Goodbye.'

I turned away and marched with dignity back to

our barbecue. And her expression, I was pleased to see, finally had changed. She looked very upset.

Served her right.

SEVEN

'I've developed the film with the competition photographs on it,' said Miss Lattimore. 'You'll have to get cracking, grade six, to print your entry pictures in time. This is your last art lesson before the school camp.'

Our grade certainly contained a lot of dense people.

'What competition?' asked Wendy Millson.

'What film?' asked Col.

'What photos?' asked Lisa.

'What's developing and printing?' asked Margeart Collins.

'You know very well what I mean,' said Miss Lattimore, and her voice took on a high-pitched brittle sound. 'The photographs we took in the playground last week for the interschool competition.'

'Oh, those,' said everyone, and went on throwing pellets of clay at each other.

'The people who want to enter for the competition may go into the dark-room and make a print from their negative,' said Miss Lattimore. 'And after it's washed and dried, mount it nicely on some cardboard, and make sure none of the glue seeps around the edges, and print your name, age, grade and school on the back, and . . .'

Most of the kids stopped listening at the first hint that the competition meant work. Barry Hollis hadn't started to listen in the first place. He was doing what he always did in art/craft, and that was see how much school property he could pinch without being caught. His cheeks were bulging with cut-out copper enamelling shapes, ready to spit out into his hankie when Miss Lattimore was looking the other way. He sold them to kids after school for five cents each.

'Barry Hollis, what's the meaning of that insolent face?' Miss Lattimore demanded angrily. 'I'm just about fed up with you wasting time in this class. Mr Nicholson said to send you over to the office if I had any more trouble with you this week. Well, what have you got to say for yourself, young man?'

Barry Hollis couldn't say anything without copper horse-shoes and little copper butterflies skittering out of his mouth if he opened it. So he just stared at Miss Lattimore right between her two eyes with this sinister look he could put on that always terrified new teachers. But Miss Lattimore had been teaching at Barringa East Primary for nearly two years, and her tolerance level for Barry Hollis had slowly increased over that period. I guess teachers just had to increase their tolerance levels with Barry Hollis, or they would have ended up in prison for murder.

'All right,' said Miss Lattimore. 'If you refuse to answer when I speak to you, you can just go over and tell Mr Nicholson you've been insolent again. No doubt he'll bear that in mind when he's finalizing the list for the grade six camp. Erica, you go with him to make sure he gets there.'

Someone always had to accompany Barry Hollis to the office, otherwise he just climbed over the fence and went home. Or he went down behind the sports shed and had a smoke, or caught the bus over to the shopping centre for a spot of shoplifting.

Barry Hollis tilted his sinister expression in my direction. I put up my hand – I was copying that from Alison Ashley – and told Miss Lattimore that I preferred not to escort him to the office all by myself. Last time I did, he tried to hang me up on one of the corridor pegs by the hood of my tracksuit.

'Very well. Alison, you go, too,' said Miss Lattimore. She gave Barry Hollis one last cold dismissing look, but while she was speaking to Alison, he'd managed to grab a stack of coloured paper and some sheets of Letraset and slide them under his shirt.

Outside in the corridor he spat out the copper shapes and put them in his pocket, where he already had some brand new tubes of epoxy resin. Then he pulled out a packet of cigarettes. 'Want a smoke?' he asked Alison, showing off.

'I'm not allowed to smoke,' she said simply.

Now most kids would never come out with a statement like that. They'd rather say, 'Oh, I gave up smoking last week.' Or, 'I don't smoke that brand.' Or, 'I've got a sore throat.' That was the first time I ever heard any kid at our school come right out and say they weren't allowed.

Even Barry Hollis looked stunned.

'Anyhow,' said Alison. 'Besides being a health hazard, cigarette smoke smells awful. I don't like being close to people who smoke.'

Barry Hollis did a peculiar thing. He put the unlit cigarette back in his pocket. It was just as well he did, because Miss Belmont came out of the staff room and wanted to know why he was being sent to the office under escort. Barry Hollis said what he always said to teachers who asked questions like that, which was, 'That's for me to know and you to find out.'

I took one look at Miss Belmont's expression and grabbed Alison by the arm and whisked her back into the art and craft room. Only fools would choose to hang around when volcanoes are about to erupt.

Then I became aware that I was actually touching Alison Ashley, the Snow Queen, and you don't touch people who are your enemy, and who sneakily come round to your house to spy on you. So I quickly took my hand away and wiped it on my skirt.

Miss Lattimore already had the dark-room set up. 'Alison and Yuk, you two can get started on your prints,' she said.

I picked up the strip of negatives and placed it in the enlarger. Shane Corbert had produced his usual blurry failure. Margeart, as well as scaring away the sparrow, had also managed to get a blobby image of her thumb. Someone else, Barry Hollis probably, had taken a picture of a bottom bending over in tight jeans. I moved the strip of negatives along and came to the one Alison had taken of the tyres.

'You can go first and get your funny little picture done,' I said. 'I like to spend a lot of time without any distractions when I work. Now, this machine is called an enlarger, and this knob here is the focuser, and this little switch is what you use to turn the red shutter on and off . . .'

'I know all that already,' said Alison Ashley. 'You're not the only person in the world who knows about photography.'

She fiddled around making test strips on different grades of paper. Then she made one large print, developed it and put it in the tray of fixer, doing all the correct things, such as handling only the corners with the tongs, and not getting one splash of chemicals out of the trays.

'It's been in long enough to have a look at it under white light,' she said.

White light, indeed! Nobody else except Miss Lattimore called it that. I switched on the overhead light and looked over her shoulder stealthily, because I certainly didn't want to give her the impression of being interested in anything that she did.

The picture was marvellous.

Everything was perfect, the shadows crisp and dark, every little detail sharp. It didn't look a bit like a snapshot of old playground equipment. It looked just like a picture you would pay a lot for if it was poster sized in a newsagency.

Miss Lattimore came in and raved about it, practically with tears of pride running down her suntan. 'It's really wonderful, Alison,' she cried ecstatically. (I'd noticed before that art/craft teachers at our school always carried on like that if anyone ever produced something that looked even vaguely artistic.) 'It's really excellent work for someone your age,' Miss Lattimore burbled. 'When it's been washed and dried, you must take it over and show Mr Nicholson.'

In fact, all the teachers at Barringa East Primary carried on like that. Every time any kid produced something that was tidy, clean, completed or even recognizable as work, they'd be sent over to show it to Mr Nicholson. Maybe the teachers felt sorry for him, having to go along to seminars with all the other principals from schools like Gilland, Edgeworth and Jacana Heights.

I felt jealous. All through my years at Barringa East Primary, from prep grade up, I'd always been the one sent to show work to Mr Nicholson. 'Right,' I thought, when they both went out to wash Alison's marvellous print. 'This is where I show Alison Ashley what real photography is all about.'

I found my negatives of bark, and projected the first one to the largest possible size. If I'd known how to project it right down on to the floor to make it poster size, even if I had to use the photo paper stuck together with sticky tape, I would have, but we weren't allowed to fiddle round too much with the enlarger.

· I moved the focusing knob to get a sharp image but nothing much happened. The negative just wouldn't come into focus. I tried all the others I'd taken, then realized with humiliation that it was because I hadn't got the distances right in the first place when I took the photos.

'Very well, then,' I thought. 'It will be an artistically blurry photograph. Anyone can take an ordinary, focused picture. Mine will be original and different.'

I used up quite a lot of paper making prints, but they didn't really look artistically blurred. They just looked like close ups of tree bark that hadn't been properly focused. However, I examined the biggest print under white light, and convinced myself that it was just like one of those big misty greeting cards you buy in shops. (Inside they have messages written in silver ink saying, 'Serenity is footprints along a solitary shore' and they cost five weeks' pocket money.)

Several people were kicking down the door and yelling it was their turn and what was I taking so long over. I hid all the wasted pieces of paper so nobody would suspect I'd run into slight technical difficulties. Then I took the print out on a paper towel to show Miss Lattimore and Alison Ashley a thing or two. All the kids came crowding round to see if they were in it. They stared at my tree bark.

'What is it?' asked Margeart.

'Skin problems,' said Sharlene.

'Leprosy,' said Colin.

'Acne and blackheads,' said Bill.

'Skin peeling off after a sunburn,' said Lisa.

'Skin on a drowned corpse that's been in the water three months,' said everyone.

'Don't be so disgusting,' said Miss Lattimore. 'At least Erica produced an entry for the competition, which is more than can be said for various other people in this grade. It's very nice, Yuk. A very nice print of . . . What exactly is it, Erica?'

Barry Hollis, back from being sorted out by Miss Belmont and Mr Nicholson, shoved his face up to my print and peered. 'It's got a dirty word written on it,' he said. 'She's taken a picture of a dirty word.'

'Barry Hollis, I have just about had enough of you,' said Miss Lattimore sternly. 'You spoil every class. You never want to learn. You're the rudest boy I ever met. You think you're being so smart, but you are just boring and tedious.'

Barry Hollis had been hearing similar observations from every adult in his life, probably since the day he was born, so he wasn't offended or anything. He turned my photograph upside down and traced across it with his finger. 'Take a look at that,' he said.

I could have died.

There, carved in large scribbled letters deep into the bark of that tree, right on the section I'd photographed, was an obscene word. Everyone began to cheer and clap and stamp their feet.

'Fancy a tree knowing that word,' said Margeart Collins dopily when Miss Lattimore quietened everyone down and was reaching in her handbag for a throat lozenge.

'I didn't notice it when I took that photo, or when I was doing the enlarging,' I said. 'I guess I had the negative in upside down. I didn't take a photo of a rude word on purpose, Miss Lattimore.'

She gave me a very disappointed, suspicious look and didn't say anything.

'I can still enter this print in the competition upside down, can't I?' I asked.

'Certainly not,' said Miss Lattimore when the Strepsil had worked enough for her voice to come back. 'It would give this school a bad name, a worse one than it has already, if any of the judges noticed. Alison's print can represent this grade from our school. And I wouldn't be at all surprised if it won a prize in its section.'

Alison Ashley, I thought, I wish something terrible would happen to you! The elastic in your pants would bust, and you'd lose them somewhere really embarrassing and public, like Monday-morning assembly. Or you'd get into a busy lift, and somehow press a whole bunch of buttons at the same time, and make the lift get stuck for about six hours with a crowd of managing directors all on their way to important meetings, and they'd know you were responsible.

I went out the front to put my rude photo in the waste-paper bin.

She came right out behind me to sharpen a pencil. I searched her navy-blue eyes for emotions, but as usual you couldn't tell what Alison Ashley was thinking. I figured she must have been feeling what I would have, if I'd been in her position. Triumph.

'Pity about your photo,' she said. 'It certainly was original. It's a shame it has to end up in the bin after all your hard work.'

Standing there batting her innocent, blue, kitten eyes and purring like a cat full of mouse. Gloating through every triumphant minute.

There is a limit to what a person can endure.

'You think you're better than anyone else in Barringa East Primary, Alison Ashley,' I said furiously. 'Stop acting so snobby and stuck up. And quit picking on people, too. You've got to be careful whom you pick on at this school.'

'Who said I was picking on anyone?'

'Let me tell you, Alison Ashley,' I said. 'I have some very powerful friends in this school who don't like me being picked on. In school hours, or out of school hours.'

'Congratulations,' she said, and tapped the pencil shavings into the bin. Then she began to sharpen the pencil at the other end. (Which just showed what a mean, ungenerous nature she had.)

'So I'm just warning you, Alison Ashley,' I said. 'If you go on showing me up all the time in school and at barbecues and everywhere, then I'll have no other alternative.'

'Than what?'

'Than to ask my best friend Barry Hollis to bash you up.'

'Well then, why don't you ask him now, Yuk?' she said pleasantly. 'He's standing right behind you.'

Eavesdropping, with his ears sticking out like lilies. He was just in the process of reacting to what I'd said about him being my best friend. His mouth was ajar with fury, and his fist bunching up into an almighty punch.

Luckily the bell rang for afternoon recess. As I didn't feel like spending it in the playground with Barry Hollis looking so dangerous, I headed for the sick bay. But Mrs Orlando wouldn't let me in, as the bed was already occupied by a kid from grade four having a very inferior migraine. So I retreated into the library and got out the copies of the two plays last year's grade six did at the annual camp.

The grade six camp was considered the highlight of the year. It was supposed to foster high ideals such as character building and team work. Every time a grade six went off to that camp, there would be a serious assembly with Mr Nicholson delivering a special annual speech. The grade sixers stood clutching their rolled-up sleeping bags and listened with respectful, obedient faces positively glowing with high ideals. Maybe because they didn't want to get left behind at the last minute.

Every year at the camp they had a drama night, and each group put on a play, and parents drove up to the camp to watch. I'd been secretly learning the star roles in those plays for weeks. It was going to be my brilliant debut into the theatre, though neither of the plays was worthy enough. They were the same tired plays Barringa East Grade Six Camp had been putting on for years. One was about King Arthur, the other about pirates, and the scripts were scribbled over with terse stage directions by desperate teachers who'd been in charge of drama at those camps. You could trace where parts had been snatched away from kids and given to others, and finally scrubbed out of the final production altogether. One year they'd apparently ended up with only two pirates on stage for the whole show, and King Arthur was killed off in Scene one, Act one.

Drama hadn't ever been a very successful subject at Barringa East Primary, but I was going to change all that.

After recess Miss Belmont handed out secret ballot forms. You had to write down the names of three people you would most like to share a room with at the camp. That was so Miss Belmont would know not to put kids who really hated each other in the same room. Everyone made a big thing out of filling in their forms, even writing on them under their desk lids, though practically everyone had already fixed up whom they were going to share rooms with months back.

I sat and stared at my ballot form. I realized that no one would write my name on their forms, and there wasn't one kid in our grade I wanted to share a room with for a whole week, either. So I put up my hand.

'Miss Belmont,' I said. 'Could I please have a single room to myself at this camp? It's this chronic insomnia I suffer from. Maybe I could stay at the camp manager's house and just come over to the camp for meals and drama rehearsals.'

'Erica Yurken,' Miss Belmont said. 'You have an exaggerated sense of your own importance. Everyone experiences insomnia at some time or another, and it's something we all have to learn to deal with. There are no single rooms available at this camp, as you'd have seen for yourself if you'd bothered to read the form properly. So kindly write down three names in the spaces, and stop being so neurotic.'

I considered all the kids in our grade without much enthusiasm. Finally I wrote down Margeart Collins's name in the first space. Although she was so dense, I guessed I could stand her for a week if I tried. I wrote Leanne Jessop's name in the second space, because it was a safe bet that she'd be overcome by homesickness the first evening, and one of the teachers would have to drive her back to Barringa East. Then I looked at the last space.

And crazily, without me doing anything at all to stop it, my hand all by itself wrote Alison Ashley.

EIGHT

On Saturday mum and Lennie went to the races. They took Jedda, who had a newspaper clipping with the names of the horses she was going to bet on underlined in red. I thought it was disgraceful, an innocent child allowed to bet her pocket money on horses.

'Erk, don't be daft. She doesn't place the bets herself,' mum said indignantly. 'That's illegal. Len puts something on for her, though mind you, she can pick a winner better than Lennie and me put together. What's going to romp home in race five, love?'

'Guinea Gold,' said Jedda. 'He always wins on a heavy track. And the distance is okay for him. He's a stayer.'

'Oh, isn't she cute?' mum cried. 'Len, did you hear what Jedda said?'

'She doesn't sound cute at all,' I said crossly. 'She sounds like a beery old derelict at the TAB.'

They invited me to go along to the races, too, but the only thing I liked doing there was watching the rich people in the members' stand. I was positive that I would have fitted into a rich, racehorse-

owning family much better than into my Barringa
East family. Sometimes I wondered if there'd been
a muddle at the hospital where I was born, and I'd
really been a posh baby belonging to someone else.
But last year when I went to visit my Aunty Val at
the same hospital, I saw straight away that rich
people wouldn't go there to have their babies.
They'd go to a private hospital. Mum always said
that the only decent thing on the menu at Barringa
Community Hospital was braised rabbit, and you
had to queue up for the showers.

I just couldn't imagine the women in the members' stand at the races eating braised rabbit or
queuing up for showers. I spent a lot of time studying the way they talked and greeted each other, and
the way they dressed. Mum got all dressed up to go
to the races, but she never did manage to look anything like those ladies. 'Wouldn't want to,' she said.
'They're crazy. Fancy having all the cash you want
to spend on clothes, and buying something as plain
as a nun's nightie.'

The dresses in the members' stand didn't look a
bit like nuns' nighties, and their wearers always had
magnificent suntans, beautiful huge sunglasses and
swoopy brimmed hats.

'I don't want to go to the races today,' I said. 'I've
got to get my things ready for the camp.' I didn't
explain that it was because I felt I really belonged
over in the members' stand instead of with mum
and Lennie and their crowd. I didn't want to hurt
her feelings.

After they left, Valjoy went off to her Saturday milkbar job. 'I won't be home for tea,' she said. 'Tell mum I'm having tea at Julie's, and then we're going to a church fellowship's young people's social.' That meant she was scheming to go to some party mum wouldn't have let her go to if she'd known anything about it.

I did my dismal weekend jobs, such as scrubbing out the bathroom basin and tub, and tidying up my part of the bedroom. It was pointless vacuuming the floor. Jedda had made it into a racecourse, using great slabs of bright-green artificial grass, like the stuff they line butcher-shop windows with. Lennie had given it to her.

Then I did my packing for the camp. Mum had got together a pile of my oldest shirts and jeans she thought would be just right for a school camp. I dumped most of them in the bottom of the ironing basket. That was the best place to hide stuff at our house, because mum thought ironing was the most boring job in the world next to cutting school lunches.

I took the suitcase into Valjoy's room and started packing properly. I packed Valjoy's blue satin shirt that tied in a knot above the navel, and her new shiny jeans, though I had to take the hems up with sticky tape. I borrowed her black transparent nightie which mum wouldn't let her wear round the house or anywhere else for that matter, and its matching transparent dressing gown that mum wouldn't let her wear, either. And a pair of patent-leather disco shoes with silver stiletto heels, and also a shoebox full of her make up. And her strapless jungle-print dress with the slit sides, though I wasn't sure if it would stay up. I also packed her bottle of Charlie perfume which she'd given up marking the levels on.

Then I filled the spaces with some of my own clothes and put the suitcase by the front door. After that I sat on my bed and sank into my usual Saturday-afternoon gloom. Life was sometimes difficult if you didn't have any friends even though you'd been going to the same school for six years. The whole dreary afternoon loomed ahead, with nothing to look at except a grass floor, and nothing to think about except what Valjoy would do to me for taking her clothes.

There was a permission form that had to be handed in on Monday, signed by our parents, and if we didn't bring it, we wouldn't even be allowed on the bus.

I opened my school bag to get it ready for mum to sign as soon as she came home from the races. And right on top of my school things was Alison Ashley's folder, with her permission form tucked inside the cover.

I turned over the spotless pages in her folder. Handwriting is supposed to reflect your personality. If it slopes backwards and is small and thin, you're a mean secretive creep. On the other hand, if it's like mine and races light heartedly over to the right-hand side of the page, it means you're generous, warm hearted, interesting and dynamic. But Alison's tidy vertical writing, neat as a scalloped picket fence, didn't give anything away. Every so often, where Miss Belmont had corrected work, there was a big red tick, or an A, or an excellent. I shut the folder jealously and glared at the stylish cover with its marbled paper and her address on a white sticker in one corner: Alison Ashley, 23 Hedge End Road, Jacana Heights.

Not Jacana Heights anymore, I thought with satisfaction. Not since they put the freeway through and you got stuck in the Barringa East Primary School zone, Alison Ashley.

She'd be in a flap about her permission note; if it wasn't signed and delivered to school on Monday morning, Miss Belmont wouldn't let her go to the camp. Good.

Not unless I took it around to her house.

And why not? I thought. I had a right to walk along Hedge End Road if I wanted to, specially as it was part of Barringa East.

I took along my secret Barry Hollis repellent in case he was roaming the streets. It was a spray bottle of really strong-smelling perfume that even Valjoy pulled a face at. It had shifted our cat when he jumped into the fridge after a frozen chicken and wouldn't come out.

I set off for Hedge End Road; Alison Ashley territory, where lawns looked like still green pools, and every house in its pretty garden had gleaming wide windows, as though the people in Hedge Road had no skeletons rattling around in their cupboards. I stopped now and then and pretended to be fixing my sandal, so I could have a good look through all those house windows. There were lounge suites with striped satin covers and velvet cushions, and Siamese cats sunning themselves, not common old evil toms like our Norm. There were coffee tables with big glass-bottle gardens on them. I could imagine what would happen if we got one of those bottle gardens at our place; it would be used as an ashtray by Lennie.

The cars parked in the driveways were all like Alison Ashley's family car; polished twentieth-century magic coaches.

I found number twenty-three and stood staring at the front door. It was the most beautiful front door I'd even seen, carved wood with amber glass panels on each side. After I'd examined it for a long time, I realized how dumb it was to feel inferior to a door, so I walked up the drive and rang the bell. A set of chimes rippled and I rang again straight away, just for the pleasure of listening to them. The door opened and Alison Ashley looked out at me.

I wished I'd tidied myself up a bit. She wore a green batik-print skirt, a silky top, and gold thongs. Her hair was hanging loosely around her shoulders, brushed smooth as a shell. She looked like an elegant mermaid.

I scowled at her. 'I found your work folder and your form for the camp,' I said. 'Somehow they got muddled up with the things in my bag.'

'Oh, thank goodness you brought it over!' she said. 'I was wondering what I was going to do. Mum wouldn't have been able to come to school early on Monday to sign another copy. Thanks, Yuk. Come in.'

'Only for a minute,' I said stiffly. 'I never have much time on Saturday afternoons. My sister's in the swimming team training for the next Olympic games, and I help coach them. I hold the stop watch and keep a clipboard record with all their times written down.'

'Do you?' said Alison. 'I was just making myself a milkshake. Want one? Only if you don't mind, we won't talk until we're in the kitchen. Mum's asleep. She has to work late tonight, so she's having a sleep now. She doesn't like ... I mean, I don't want to wake her up. The kitchen's this way, Erica.'

Light filtered through the amber-glass panels and it was like being inside an aquarium. Alison floated down the hallway, with her long gold hair streaming behind, and I floundered along after her, trying not to make a noise. She swam off the carpet and on to cool green tiles, and shut the kitchen door behind us. I didn't know kitchens outside magazines could look like that. There were trailing ferns in baskets, copper pots hanging on the walls, and about a million dollars worth of electrical appliances.

'Strawberry or chocolate milkshake?' she asked.

'I thought you said you never ate junk food.'

'Home made milkshakes aren't junk food. Mum

buys special flavourings without sugar.' She pressed a button on an enormous blender and it hummed softly, though I was expecting something that size to sound like a pneumatic drill. She poured out these marvellous milkshakes, with a metre of foam on the top, into two tall glasses. They were very plain glasses, but it was obvious they hadn't ever contained peanut butter or instant coffee. Alison rinsed out the blender and put it upside down to drain on a paper towel. Then she wiped the bench top, even though it was perfectly clean, and finally she sat down opposite me and drank her milkshake. 'My mother's a bit fussy,' she said. 'I always have to clean things up straight away. I suppose it's the easiest way, really, to keep a house looking tidy.'

I wondered suspiciously if she'd said those last words in insulting capital letters, but her eyes were as innocent as daisies. I drank my milkshake and inspected the kitchen. Then I looked from all that gleaming splendour at Alison Ashley and climbed inside her mind and inspected her thoughts. 'Go ahead and look, Erica Yurken,' they clearly said. 'That dishwasher over there is the latest model. So is the fridge. Only, my mother BOUGHT it, she doesn't have to win kitchen equipment in a football club raffle. Would you like to have a look inside it? Maybe you're hungry. Oh, sorry, can't help you, we never have junk food and frozen pies in our fridge. I could run out the back and get some grass clippings and pop them in a plastic bag.'

'I'm certainly glad we haven't got a dishwasher

at our house,' I said tersely. 'I feel really sorry for people who wash up with a dishwasher. They kill family conversations. We have terrific fun at our place while one's washing and one's drying and the others are putting the dishes away.'

Actually, it wasn't a bit like that. Mum washed up every night. She had to stay in the kitchen to stop Valjoy, Harley, Jedda and me from murdering each other. Cleaning up always seemed to bring out the worst in our characters. (Harley, it's your turn to dry up, you big slob! Mum, make Jedda stop giving Norm the saucepans to lick out! It is not my turn! Keep your nails to yourself! Take that and that and that!)

'Yes,' I said, eyeing Alison's mother's sparkling white dishwasher with loathing sprung from jealousy. 'I'd hate it if mum bought a dishwasher. We have really interesting times over the washing up at our place. We play word games.'

'Do you?' asked Alison. 'You mean like I Spy?'

'Certainly not. We play this intellectually challenging game called Hats.'

'How does it go?'

'Everyone has to think of a hat in turn, such as a police helmet or a nurse's cap, only it's got to be something different each turn. And if they can't think of one by the count of ten, they have to drop out.'

'It sounds fun,' said Alison politely.

'It's a very witty game,' I said. 'When my father was in the Antarctic gathering rock specimens for the museum, all the men stationed there used to play Hats when there was a blizzard on and they couldn't leave the tents. My father was a world expert on rocks.'

'I though you said he was a test pilot,' said Alison Ashley.

'He was a geologist as well,' I said crossly. I watched her clean the glasses. First she washed them in warm water. Then she rinsed them in cold, wiped them with one cloth, polished them with another. Then she put them neatly away in a cupboard. I wondered why she didn't ever fall asleep from exhaustion at school, if she had to work like that every day of her life.

'Haloes and bee-keeper nets,' she said suddenly.

'What?'

'Bank robber balaclavas and Viking helmets with horns sticking out at the sides.'

I was very annoyed with her for listing all those hats straight off like that without permission, especially as they were ones I hadn't ever thought of. The hat game was my own private invention which I played by myself when I couldn't get to sleep. We certainly never played it as a family around the sink while washing up. Everyone was always too busy yelling at each other.

'Pirate hat,' I said.

'Fireman's helmet,' said Alison Ashley.

'Riding cap.'

'Baby's bonnet.'

'Surgeon's operating cap.'

'Diamond tiara.'

'Those lace things Spanish ladies wear on their heads.'

'You mean mantillas,' said Alison Ashley. 'Cafeteria lady's hat.'

'I was just about to say mantilla. I knew those lace things were called that. Red Indian feathers. There, beat that one.'

'Executioner's hood with slit eyes,' said Alison Ashley.

'I don't feel in the mood for playing Hats right now,' I said. 'It often makes me feel depressed when I do. It reminds me that my father's not here to join in.'

'You're not the only one who hasn't got a dad,' said Alison abruptly. 'Mine's not around, either. They got divorced last year.'

'That's not as bad as losing your father in a tragic plane crash,' I said. 'You can still go and visit him, can't you?'

'Not when he's gone off to Canada and hardly ever writes or anything.'

'At least you've still got your mother.'

Alison didn't say anything. Her face had its shutters down, and it was clear that she regretted allowing me to catch a glimpse of her private life. 'I'd invite you in to my room to play records or play Scrabble or something,' she said. 'But we'd better not. I don't want to wake up my mother. She works very long hours at the weekend. We could sit in the family room instead.'

The family room was bigger than our kitchen and living room stuck together. It had off-white carpet, which seemed to me to be just plain showing off, though probably Alison never ever did anything or went anywhere messy enough to get dirt on the soles of her shoes. There was a huge television against one wall, but Alison said we'd better not turn it on because her mother was a very light sleeper. I sat in a cane hanging chair. All my life I'd wanted to sit in one of those and gyrate, but now I had the opportunity, I found myself sitting just as quietly and decorously as Alison, with my hands folded in my lap.

I looked around the family room. It was really beautiful, with massed pot plants at the window. There was a coffee table holding one big book about art, and a white telephone on a pedestal thing in a corner, and a white fleecy rug in the exact centre of the carpet. In the whole room there wasn't one thing out of line, or one speck of dust. Even the divan cushions looked as though they'd been set there by computer. It was definitely not a room to gyrate in.

Family room wasn't a proper title for it, unless it was for a family of shop-window models. I couldn't imagine people eating apples there, or slippered feet resting next to bowls of hot popcorn on the shiny coffee-table top. The whole room made me conscious of my terrible old ripped jeans. Mum had stapled the rip together because she hated mending so much.

Tears in Alison Ashley's clothes were probably invisibly mended at a dry cleaners, though most likely she never tore her clothes in the first place. I figured that her mother might be a nursing sister, from the odd hours she worked. That would explain why Alison always looked so germ free and why she always ate healthy wholesome food and had sterilized-looking fingernails.

'Which hospital does she work at?' I asked.

'Who?'

'Your mother.'

'She's not a nurse. She's in partnership with someone. They own a restaurant.'

'Like a pizza parlour?'

'No, it's a proper licensed restaurant with waiters. It's lovely inside. They have silver candlesticks on the tables and velvet chairs. Mum's the hostess there and she helps order the food and run it and everything. She's very good at things like that.'

I had an embarrassing memory of me telling her that I was allowed to work as a waitress at mum's hotel and serve alcoholic drinks. And all the time she must have realized, with her sneakily concealed knowledge, that it wouldn't be possible for me to do any such thing.

'I'd better go,' I said with dignity, getting out of the hanging chair. 'I've got to go down to the racetrack and get my mother's friend's horses loaded on the float.'

'Oh,' said Alison. 'What about the Olympic swimming team?'

'I do that every second Saturday,' I said. 'I just remembered that today is my racetrack Saturday. The Olympic team's not till next weekend.'

'Oh. Well, you can go out the back and round the side if you like. Thanks for bringing back my folder. See you on Monday, then.'

'Yeah, Monday.'

We went through a laundry, the first one I ever saw that had colour-coordinated electrical equipment. There was an enormous clothes dryer, so probably Alison Ashley had never been hollered at for forgetting to run out and bring in the sheets before it rained. There was a patio with redwood garden furniture and a door to a double garage. As well as all the usual things you see in a garage, there was a bicycle, Alison Ashley sized, and a shelf stacked with sports gear. My eyes skittered along the shelf, filing things under a mental heading of 'Things to be jealous about where Alison Ashley is concerned.' There were skis, and roller skates, the expensive white-boot kind, and a new basketball in a plastic bag. And a fabulous skateboard that looked as though it was never used.

I took it down and flipped the wheels around. 'Your driveway would be fantastic for a skateboard,' I said. 'You're nuts keeping this up on a shelf. Fancy having a sloping driveway and not making use of it. I bet I could coast down to the street corner without having to stop once. Want to see?'

'No, I don't,' said Alison. 'You'll . . .'

I balanced and pushed out into that lovely curving driveway.

'. . . wake up my mother,' said Alison.

What a stupid place to have an orange tree, growing in a clay pot beside the front steps! I picked myself up and inspected a long graze on one elbow, but unfortunately it didn't need a tourniquet. (Just once in my life I would have liked to get a cut that needed a tourniquet, just to see what it felt like.) The graze didn't even really need a band-aid, but one couldn't be too careful about physical injuries, so I turned round to ask Alison if I could borrow one. With all the expensive stuff in their house, they might even have an operating theatre tucked away somewhere.

Alison was standing quite still, wearing her locked-up expression, and she was being told off by her mother through a front-room window.

'. . . selfish,' I heard, not being one to pass up an opportunity to eavesdrop. 'Incredibly selfish. You know very well how demanding that job is . . . I particularly asked you, Alison. Clattering about, and who on earth have you got out there, anyhow?'

'No one,' Alison said quickly. 'I mean, it's just a kid from school. Nobody, really.'

I left without a band-aid, in insulted fury. So that was what she thought of me – nobody! Too ashamed of the way I talked, of the way I looked, to introduce me to her mother.

I found this stone by the footpath and kicked it all the way up Hedge End Road and into the streets of Barringa East. And every time I kicked it, I said, 'Drop dead, Alison Ashley! See if I care, Alison Ashley! We'll see who's nobody!'

NINE

There is one thing you certainly can't hide in an excursion bus, and that is that you haven't got a best friend. When all the other best friends had paired off, Miss Belmont said, 'Why are you still roaming around, Erica? There's a perfectly good seat next to Alison. I expect all of you to remain in those seats until we reach the camp, and I don't want any unseemly behaviour from anyone, such as rude signals out of the windows at police cars.'

While she was delivering her standard lecture on bus etiquette, I slid into the seat and gave Alison Ashley a look of utter loathing and hatred.

'What's the matter?' she said.

'Utter loathing and hatred,' I said. 'I wouldn't even be on the same bus as you, let alone the same seat, if I could have caught a virus in time. But I suppose in your eyes I'm not here anyhow. I'm nowhere, according to you. Nobody.'

'I didn't mean it like that,' Alison said. 'It's just that my mother has a very bad temper. I didn't want you to get yelled at for making the noise with the skateboard and waking her up. So that's why I sort of hustled you off.'

'A likely story!' I said. (Which is a very dramatic statement and one that I'd always been dying to have the opportunity of using.) 'A likely story, Alison Ashley!'

'Please yourself, then,' she said calmly. 'If you don't want to talk, then don't. It won't bother me. I've got the window to look out of.'

There's not much at all to look at from the inside seat of a bus except kids' feet sticking out into the aisle. Nicole and Bev behind us were having a conversation, but it wasn't worth the trouble of eavesdropping. It was too complicated. All they ever talked about was how horrible Karen and Vicky were. Only they had a bust up every five minutes and changed sides, and then it was Karen telling Nicole how horrible Bev and Vicky were. It seemed to me that our grade had more boring people in it than any other grade in any other school in the country. Irritating, as well as boring. We hadn't been on the road for more than ten minutes before a whole lot of kids began to say they were hungry and could they eat their packed lunches.

Margeart in front of us called out to Miss Belmont that she was carsick, even though we hadn't been round one bend yet. Miss Belmont told her briskly that it was all in her mind, and to play some game as a distraction. 'But the sports equipment's locked away in the boot,' said Margeart.

Alison Ashley, that traitor, piped up and said she

knew a marvellous game called Hats. I folded my arms and listened while Alison Ashley, traitor and thief, explained the rules of Hats to everyone in the nearby seats. Margeart was hopeless at it. They let her have first try and she thought for ages and said, 'Hair'. Then Alison explained the rules again patiently, and Margeart said, 'Hair curlers.' The kids who were waiting their turn let her pass out of desperation. When her turn came round again she said, 'My nan's pink umbrella.' And next turn after that she couldn't think of anything at all.

Bev and Karen and Vicky and Nicole joined in, and before we reached the hills where the camp was, most of the bus was playing Hats. Except me. I sat and wondered if I could somehow hire a barrister and take Alison Ashley to court for theft. There was only one consolation – none of the kids in our grade came anywhere near my standard of playing. Except maybe Alison. All the others said corny things like 'sunhat' and 'school hat'.

'Coronet,' said Alison Ashley, winning her fifth game in a row.

'I suppose you think you'd look pretty good in one,' I said grimly. 'What a nerve you've got, playing my game without asking! That game's never played outside my family.'

'I thought you said they played it at the South Pole,' said Alison.

After Hats everyone sang football songs and when we finally got to the camp, the driver looked as though he could use a Disprin. So I offered him one of mine.

'Erica,' said Miss Belmont sharply. 'You were told at assembly that all medicines had to be handed over to Mrs Wentworth who's in charge of first aid on this camp. Just what else have you got in that bag?'

I had to hand over all the medical supplies I'd brought along for emergencies. My king-sized box of band-aids, a wide elastic bandage in case I was lucky enough to sprain an ankle, cherry-flavoured cough medicine, a large bottle of calamine lotion in case of sunburn, and antihistamine ointment for insect bites. Miss Belmont made me give her the whole lot and told me off in front of the bus driver. Everyone else shuffled their feet and glared because they wanted to hop off the bus and explore the camp. Except Mrs Wentworth who said she wanted a nice hot cup of tea before she did anything.

We unloaded the bus and carried all the suitcases and sleeping bags up to the building. Then Miss Belmont read out the room list. I was put in with Margeart and Leanne Jessop. And Alison Ashley. 'I certainly didn't write your name on my ballot form,' I hissed. 'There's no way I would have chosen you to share a room with for a whole week. Get that straight.'

'Well then, I didn't put your name down on mine,' she said. 'You needn't think I did. Who'd want to share a room with a cactus?'

Our room was down the far end of the girls' part of the building. It had four bunk beds, only the beds weren't over each other, the space under the high ones was for hanging up our things. 'I have to have a firm solid mattress because of my fused vertebra,' I said.

Margeart said she didn't think we were allowed to meddle around with electricity on the camp. Leanne didn't say anything. She just sat on her suitcase looking homesick though we hadn't been at the camp for more than a quarter of an hour.

'You haven't got a fused vertebra,' said Alison.

'That's all you know. When I was eight I fell off a bolting horse. I was rounding up cattle on my uncle's cattle station in the Northern Territory. I was dragged through a mangrove swamp, but luckily the horse stopped right on the edge of the cliff. Even so they had to get an army helicopter in to rescue me. And that's why I have to have the best mattress in the room.'

'My nan has a bad back, too,' said Margeart. 'It's called lumbago. I never knew kids our age could catch lumbago.'

I thought grudgingly that it mightn't be such a terrible thing having Alison in that room. At least she listened properly. We unrolled our sleeping bags and spread them on the bunks. Only, as you might have guessed, Alison Ashley hadn't brought along a sleeping bag. She had a quilt, a fitted sheet, and matching pillowcase patterned all over with pale-blue flowers.

'This is supposed to be a camp,' I said. 'That fancy quilt looks really dumb and out of place.'

'I didn't have a sleeping bag,' said Alison. 'We never go camping, and I didn't know anyone I could borrow one from. Mum said it was a waste to buy one just for a week.'

I had an old sleeping bag of Harley's, from when he was a boy scout about a hundred years ago, but I turned it over so she wouldn't see the 3rd Barringa East label. 'This one I've got is very valuable,' I said. 'It looks old and battered, but that's because it was used on the first expedition to climb Mount Everest.'

'I suppose you're going to tell us you're related to Sir Edmund Hillary next,' said Alison.

I opened the lid of my suitcase. The moment had come to squash Alison Ashley firmly for all that week at camp, and maybe firmly enough to keep her squashed for the rest of the year. I began to take out Valjoy's clothes. Slowly, one item at a time, with great dramatic flair. And before I even had her blue satin shirt draped over a hanger, there was Karen and Vicky and that crowd milling around in the doorway, with their lower lips drooping nearly down to their kneecaps from jealousy.

'Wow!' they said. 'Check the clothes! Oooh, those patent-leather shoes! And the jungle-print dress! Can we come in and look, Yuk?'

'Can I borrow those beaut shoes to wear to dinner?' asked Bev.

'Can I wear those shiny jeans just once while we're up here?' asked Karen.

Leanne Jessop didn't say anything. She was blubbing all over her sleeping-bag cover which she hadn't even untied yet because she was so homesick. Alison didn't say anything, either. She just sat on her continental quilt and watched me hang up Valjoy's clothes.

'Geeee! Just look at the nightie and negligee!' cried Vicky. 'Can I wear them one morning at breakfast?'

I unpacked Valjoy's make up and perfume and arranged them along the little table under the window, pushing aside Leanne's Raggedy Ann doll (fancy bringing such a thing to camp) and the instruction sheet Margeart's mother had printed in large block letters with simple instructions to get her safely through the week. Such as: change shoes if you get them wet in creek; don't go near creek without teacher; open zipper of sleeping bag before getting into it for the night; take off pj's before putting jeans on in morning.

Then I pushed the empty suitcase under the bed and lay on Harley's tatty old sleeping bag. 'I hope I've left you enough room, Alison,' I said. 'I didn't really mean to take up so much of the hanging space.'

The audience had grown in size, due to Karen and Vicky and Bev telling everyone along the corridor about my clothes. Kids kept looking in the door and asking if they could borrow this and that. It was lovely and I just lay there and gloated.

Then Alison Ashley quietly unpacked her clothes and hung them up. The coat hangers she'd brought along weren't old wire ones from dry cleaning; hers were all padded and crocheted. Last of all, she unpacked her dressing gown.

It was of royal-blue silk, with gold-embroidered peach blossoms, butterflies and birds over every centimetre of it, and it was lined with gold. It was magnificent; a beautiful, exotic shimmering kimono. I looked at it and realized with despair that all the stuff hanging up on my side of the clothes rack, all Valjoy's clothes, were absolutely dreadful and yuk to match my name!

I also realized that the spotlight had shifted and was now fair and square on Alison Ashley.

'Why, Alison, what a lovely dressing gown!' said Mrs Wentworth, coming along the corridor. 'You're a very lucky girl to own such a beautiful thing.'

Alison Ashley had the nerve to look politely surprised that all the kids, and even a teacher, were even noticing it. She just draped it carelessly over the foot of her bed. 'My mother bought it overseas somewhere,' she said. 'But it's not all that useful, really. It's not warm enough for winter, and it's a bit hot in summer. Can I help you with any jobs, Mrs Wentworth, now I've finished unpacking?'

I was left alone, brooding. She did it on purpose,

I thought, just to show me up. She probably got her mother to nip overseas by jet to buy that dressing gown specially for this camp.

Miss Belmont summoned everyone to a meeting in the main room. 'I don't want you lounging around on that bed being lazy all this week, Erica,' she said, frowning. 'That's not the idea of a camp at all. If you didn't have anything to do, you could have offered to help Mrs Wentworth. Alison's been helping unload the sports equipment. Perhaps some of her consideration might rub off onto you over the next five days.'

Then she saw the cosmetics on the table and frowned some more. Then she saw Valjoy's clothes and frowned a lot more. She spent the next five minutes putting Valjoy's clothes and cosmetics into a plastic bag and tying a big bossy knot on the top. 'The very idea, bringing clothes like these along!' she said. 'They're not even yours, either, I can tell by the size. You can collect all this from me at the end of the camp. I can see I'll have to keep a very close eye on your behaviour during the week.'

She sounded peppery, and so did the lecture she delivered in the main room. It was all about the camp being a time when we were away from home and relying on each other and ourselves, and how the teachers were all giving up a week away from their families with no overtime pay, either, and how, if anyone stepped out of line, Miss Belmont would phone Mr Nicholson and he'd come up in his car and take them home in disgrace. (That was said on the camp every year; other grade sixes had come back and said so, but it never happened. Maybe the teacher in charge had to learn a set threatening speech.)

We were put into two groups with a male and female group leader, and that was going to be the group we stayed with each day for activities. I was disgusted to find that I was in the same group as Alison Ashley. The pep talk took a long time. Barry Hollis got into trouble twice while it was going on. Mr Kennard yelled at him for unhitching the fire extinguisher from the wall, and Mrs Wentworth told him off for climbing the piano. Mrs Wentworth wasn't very good at telling people off. They borrowed her from the prep grade for school camps because she was motherly. She used to say these really dumb sweet things to kids such as, 'Now, dear, I know you wouldn't tell me a lie, so if you say it wasn't you who threw that icy pole wrapper down there, I believe you.' (Even if the kid had a vivid green icy-pole moustache all round their mouth.) But everyone liked her a lot because she always remembered if it was your birthday, and she listened politely to boring stories kids told her about their cat's six kittens and what they were going to call each one. She said to Barry Hollis, 'Barry, be a good boy and don't walk along the piano keys like that.' Barry Hollis didn't take any notice, so Miss Belmont roared across the room, 'Barry Hollis, I'll count till three!' and he meekly got down at two and shut the piano lid.

Actually, they hadn't planned to take Barry Hollis along (this I'd overheard at school while I was in the sick bay), but his mother came up to school and begged and pleaded because she needed the week's break away from him while the doctor was trying to get her off sedatives. And Mr Nicholson felt so sorry for her he said Barry could go to the camp, as long as he promised to behave. There really wasn't much point making Barry Hollis promise anything, because he wouldn't keep it, but Miss Belmont was substituting capably with her laser beam voice.

We were given our camp programme, with each day's timetable of activities; bushcraft with Mr Kennard, art and craft with Miss Lattimore, drama with Miss Wentworth, and sport with Miss Belmont. And then we had to go for a long healthy walk before tea.

At first it was great walking along winding country roads past old weatherboard houses with verandas and iron roofs, and horses gazing at us over fences, and dogs charging out (but reversing direction as soon as they made the combined acquaintance of Barry Hollis and Miss Belmont).

Mrs Wentworth walked behind us, goodnaturedly carrying everyone's pullovers. She had to hold Leanne's hand to get her past every magpie we met. Then Margeart Collins lost her shoe. She didn't know how or where she lost it. One minute she had it on, and the next minute she was hopping along on one foot calling out urgently for Miss Belmont to stop. Everyone went back and hunted for it, and Miss Belmont said crossly, 'How can anyone possibly lose a shoe without even noticing? Margaret Collins, I just hope this camp teaches you better co-ordination.'

Mrs Wentworth volunteered to sit at the side of the road and mind Margeart and wait for the others to climb to the top of the mountain Miss Belmont had selected for our hike. By then a lot of kids were looking very tired. Kids from Barringa East didn't get all that much practice bushwalking. In fact all the walking they ever did was nipping down to the milkbar or the fish and chip shop after school, and dodging Barry Hollis. So a lot of people flopped down beside Mrs Wentworth and refused to get up.

'These children will have to do much better, won't they, Mr Kennard?' Miss Belmont said fiercely. 'This is only a short stroll, because it's the first day and we had to get unpacked and settled in. But starting from tomorrow, we'll be walking ten times this distance every day. I've never seen such a lazy lot of boys and girls. Well then, those people with no pride may stay back and be minded by Mrs Wentworth as though they belong in prep, and the ones who are willing to join in the proper spirit of this camp can walk with me and Mr Kennard and Miss Lattimore to the top.'

I felt sorry for Mr Kennard and Miss Lattimore. You could tell they'd rather be sitting down somewhere with a cup of coffee and a cigarette, but they had to look enthusiastic and agree with Miss Belmont because she was running the camp.

I wanted to stay back with Mrs Wentworth, but Alison Ashley was still on her feet. I looked at her. Everyone else by that time had half the road on their jeans, and muddy bark in their hair, and hot red sweaty faces. But Alison looked no different from what she did at school. Spotless and confident. And also genuinely eager to climb right to the top of that mountain. So naturally I had to as well. Everyone not yet crippled heaved themselves along after the teachers. But Alison Ashley walked jauntily, not even puffing, no doubt because of those vitamins she was always eating for lunch.

When we got to the top, the view wasn't all that marvellous. Just trees, and other hills with more trees on them, and the school camp about a thousand kilometres away on the horizon. I didn't have the strength to look at the view, anyhow. Even my eyelids were stiff and exhausted. I sank down, groaning, with all the other groaning kids. Alison was the only one who didn't. She walked all over the mountain top taking pictures of the view with the school camera. She didn't look tired, and she still wasn't puffing. I gazed at her with bitter, black hatred.

All the good things in the world lavished on her, beauty, nice manners, braininess, lovely clothes, photography skills, long eyelashes, A's in her work folder, a house in Hedge End Road, Kyle Grammar School, the world's healthiest pair of lungs.

It just wasn't fair.

And added to all that she owned the most glamorous dressing gown in the world as well.

TEN

We had to have a shower when we got back from the hike, then Kangas, the group I was in, had to go over and set the tables in the hall. But I was so tired I sat down in the shower recess under the warm spray and had a nap instead.

'Erica, are you by any chance trying to get out of dining-room duties?' Miss Belmont demanded, thumping on the door. I dragged on some clean clothes, combed my wet hair with my fingers and went over to the hall. Barry Hollis was already standing outside in disgrace.

'I don't know why you bothered to come on this camp,' I said. 'You haven't got any idea how to behave in company.'

'Only came along to see the action tonight,' he said, 'First night of camp, that's when the Basin Skins come up the mountain and give this place a going over. Always do, every year. Real tough lot, the Basin Skins, tougher than the Eastside Boys even. They sneak in when everyone's asleep and help themselves to trannies and any cash left lying around.'

'Rubbish,' I said. 'Last year's grade six always spread that old story about the Basin Skins, just to scare the next lot coming up here. They don't even exist.'

'As if you'd know. About midnight, that's when they strike. Year before last they tattooed my brother's forehead without even waking him up. This place is haunted, too, did you know? Something real peculiar comes up out of the creek and claws at the windows, soon as it gets dark. That's how come our school can afford it here. We're their only customers. No other school in the State's game enough to come to this place. Too dangerous. And that room you're in at the end, that's where the murder happened. Peel back the rug and you can see the bloodstains. Funny things happen in there. Dunno why they bung poor innocent kids in there. Cruel, really. Bet you start bawling and wanting to go home tonight.'

'Don't be ridiculous,' I said coldly. I went into the hall and was told off by Mr Kennard because everyone else had already finished setting the tables. Mr Kennard said that I didn't have the proper camping spirit. 'I couldn't help being late,' I said. 'While I was having a shower my hair got caught up in the holes in the spray thing. I had to prise it off with a nail file.'

The camp manager, who was also the cook, stuck

his head through the serving hatch and said, 'You kids aren't allowed to go messing around with any of the fittings in this camp. You just remember that, young lady.'

It wasn't fair, being told off for something I hadn't done which I couldn't deny now I'd already told Mr Kennard I had. The camp manager rang the bell and everyone came over. Barry Hollis was allowed out of exile, and Kangas had to go around and serve out the food.

When I finished taking bowls of tomato soup around, nobody had saved me a seat at their table. The only spot left was down at the end table where there were only boys with uncouth manners. They all yakked on about the bridge they were going to build over the creek and I could have been invisible for all the notice they took of me.

I suddenly realized that I hadn't ever been away from home before. Not even for one night. For as long as I could remember, evenings had always meant mum laughing at things on the telly, Valjoy nattering on the phone, the fridge door being opened and shut, Harley's and mum's and Valjoy's friends dropping in, and the cat curled up in a self-satisfied bundle on the end of my bed. A familiar, soothing ritual I'd always taken for granted.

None of that tonight. Instead, the Basin Skins creeping in through the camp windows after transistors and kid's pocket money. Maybe it was true. Russell Griggs who was in grade six last year reckoned he found all his clothes chucked around the room and BEWARE written on the window with mud.

I looked furtively around at the other tables. All the other kids seemed really excited about being away from home. They were tucking into their food and earbashing the teacher who was sitting at their table. (There wasn't a teacher at ours. Probably they'd given it a miss on account of Barry Hollis sitting there.) No one else in the whole big echoey dining hall looked even faintly homesick. Not even sooky Leanne, but she was being mothered by Mrs Wentworth who was buttering a slice of bread for her and cutting off the crusts.

I tasted some of my soup but something peculiar was happening to my throat. It felt lined with cement, like when you get a strepthroat. Usually I thought having a strepthroat quite interesting because of the possibility of it turning out to be tonsilitis. I'd always felt cheated that it was Valjoy instead of me who had her tonsils out. But that lumpy sore throat I had on the first night of camp was definitely not interesting. It was terrible.

And there was this stinging, burning sensation behind my eyes, exactly like conjunctivitis, and I felt keyed up and nervous, as though I was coming down with a temperature. I sat at the table having all these interesting symptoms, and none of them gave me any enjoyment at all.

'Chuck over the salt,' said Colin. 'How many times do we have to ask?'

I passed it along the table silently, because I could hardly locate my voice beneath the cement.

'Yuk's bawling,' Barry Hollis hooted. 'Hey look, a big fat tear just plopped in her soup.'

'I am not bawling,' I snarled. 'For your information, I'm allergic to tomato soup. I always get runny eyes if there's tomato soup around.' I pushed the bowl aside and concentrated very hard on the menu chalked up outside the kitchen. Tomato soup, sausages, chips and salad, creamed apple rice. The chalked letters trembled and shifted as though I was reading them under water. I put my elbows on the table and my head in between my hands, and stretched the skin of each temple tightly. My eyes felt slitted and uncomfortable, but at least no tears could bust out.

I was supposed to get up and help clear away the soup bowls and bring around the next course, but I thought if I stayed quiet and hunched up like that, nobody would notice I was missing. Alison Ashley was being efficient enough for both of us, anyhow. Some dopey kids on duty were making trips with just one single bowl or one spoon in their hands. But Alison cleared each table intelligently by stacking the soup bowls with the spoons in a tidy nest on the top one. She came to our table and I shot her an inscrutable oriental look from under my stretched eyelids. She put a big bowl of salad in the centre of our table, and a plate of sausages and chips down in front of me.

'Thank you,' I said icily, and I must say that even

though I was so upset, my voice achieved the exact tone I wanted, that of a rich haughty lady thanking a parlour maid for picking up a dropped fan.

'Are you all right, Yuk?' Alison asked uncertainly. 'Want to come and sit at our table? We could all move up a place.'

'Whatever for? I'm quite happy sitting here,' I said. Two fat sausages and a pile of chips on my plate, reminding me achingly of home. The sort of meal mum dished up because it was quick and easy and could be eaten in front of the TV. I put my knife and fork down.

'Want me to get one of the teachers?' Alison said. She said it into one of those clear sudden silences that happen sometimes, for instance when plates of food are set in front of kids and they all have their mouths full. 'What's the matter, Erica?' she asked, and the words bounced and echoed all around the silence in the hall, and everyone stopped chewing and turned their heads to stare over half a fat sausage speared on their forks. 'Are you homesick?' asked Alison Ashley. 'Is that what the matter is? Would you like me to get you a paper tissue? Why are you crying?'

It was awful. Everywhere I looked I met curious eyes, all shamelessly gawking, the way kids always do when someone bawls in public. And I knew at once that Alison Ashley had chosen that exact moment when the hall was silent, just to embarrass me. That was the underhand scheming way she worked.

So I jumped up and dumped the bowl of salad right over her head.

Even then she didn't look undignified, though everyone was really staring by then. She just took the bowl off her head and began to gather up bits of lettuce and radish and replace them neatly in the bowl. As composed and dignified as though she was shaking off a few raindrops.

'Erica Yurken, you can go to your room for that sort of behaviour,' Miss Belmont boomed across the hall. 'I will not allow silly horseplay during meals.'

I went across to the deserted dormitory block and sat on my Mount Everest sleeping bag and considered. I could pack my things and leave, only I didn't know how to get to the nearest railway station. I didn't think any of the teachers would drive me home, either, even if I asked nicely. They all looked too tired from Miss Belmont's mountain climbing.

I could pretend to be taken seriously ill with gallstones, only I couldn't remember which side the gall bladder was on. Or I could feign a different minor illness every morning and spend the whole five days in bed, only the thought of lying there for five days having to look at Alison Ashley's magnificent dressing gown was too depressing.

It was lonesome being in the building all by myself. Birds walked scratchily up and down on the roof, and it sounded like people prowling around up there in the dusk. The Basin Skins. I began to feel nervous, but I knew it was probably only a matter of time before Barry Hollis was sent over in disgrace to his room, too. Back at school he never ever got through one lunchtime without being sent out in disgrace. At least I'd have human company, even if Barry Hollis barely made the rating. Sure enough, he soon came clumping down the concrete steps from the dining hall. I watched him through the window. He stopped at the terrace and switched everyone's wellington boots into a jumble of odd pairs, filling some with gravel, before going into his room.

When everyone else came back from the dining hall, I had to find Miss Belmont and say I was sorry about the salad, even though I wasn't. 'I can't think what came over you, trying to start a fight with Alison the first night of camp,' Miss Belmont said. 'Especially when you both asked on your ballot forms to be put in the same room. I'm certainly not going to change anyone around now. One of the purposes of this camp is for all of you to learn how to get along with each other. So just don't let me have any more trouble from you, Erica, or I'll telephone Mr Nicholson to come straight up and drive you home.'

Alison Ashley didn't even mention the salad. She just went off to the bathroom and washed her hair and came out smelling of expensive hair conditioner instead of mayonnaise.

Miss Belmont organized an evening of team games which we all had to play before we were allowed to go to bed. She had a piercing whistle on a medieval chain slung around her neck. We played games like passing balloons along on the ends of straws, and getting into clumps of numbers which Miss Belmont signalled with shattering blasts of her whistle.

People were yawning, but Miss Belmont wouldn't excuse anyone, not even the other three teachers. Miss Lattimore looked bored as well as exhausted. She hadn't wanted to come along to the camp. From the sick bay I had heard her having a fight with Mr Nicholson in his office about it. She'd threatened to quit the Education Department and earn a living making macrame flowerpot hangers for craft shops. But since none of the other teachers on the staff, except Mrs Wentworth, wanted to come to the camp, Miss Lattimore had to give in. Mr Kennard didn't have any choice. He was straight out of teachers' college.

At 9.30 Miss Belmont had to wind up the games – people had fallen asleep and Barry Hollis was miming a stripper. With one last piercing screech of her whistle, she sent us all to bed.

Immediately everyone found new vigorous energy and excitement because they were sleeping away from home. There were midnight feasts on in every room, only we held them at 10 p.m. because lights had to be out by 10.30. Even Alison Ashley had brought along food. (Some sugarless muesli cookies and an apple, and as soon as she finished eating them, she cleaned her teeth again).

The midnight feast didn't cheer Leanne up. She

sniffed and bawled so much from homesickness that Mrs Wentworth let her sleep on the spare bed in her room. Margeart couldn't find any of the supplies she'd bought for the feast. I helped her search through all her things, even in her sleeping bag and in the battery compartment of her torch, though she hadn't ever realized the lid came off. Then she remembered where she'd packed all her midnight feast things. In her desk at school.

At exactly 10.30 Miss Belmont switched off the lights. Then she, Miss Lattimore, Mrs Wentworth and Mr Kennard went into the teachers' sitting room which was next to our room, carrying cups of coffee. I put my ear against the wall, but as there was solid brick in between you couldn't hear a word. It seemed a pity, because teachers' conversations must be much more interesting when they are away on a school camp than in a staff room with the Principal present.

Alison fell asleep instantly without any trouble at all. Margeart got her pillow stuck in her sleeping-bag zipper. She thought the pillow was supposed to fit inside the hood, but once I got her straightened out, she went right off to sleep, too. And snored. I rolled my socks up into earpads and put my pillow and a spare blanket over my head, but nothing would block out the sound of Margeart's snoring. I lay for hours suffering from insomnia and homesickness and night terrors. I listened to Margeart's snoring, and the scraping noises on the roof that sounded like the Basin Skins trying to get in with a tin opener. A Basin Skin crawled along the roof and then back to the other end, no doubt hampered by a length of bicycle chain and a flick knife. Bushes outside the window moved like machetes being rattled. The Basin Skin on the roof was joined by the rest of the gang, and they scuttled and pattered all over the roof.

Margeart didn't miss one beat in her snoring, and Alison Ashley slept like an angel on a cloud. But I crept out of bed and constructed a booby trap under the window. It was made from two chairs upended on the table, with a stretched windcheater tied to the rungs as a trip rope.

I started to think about home and mum, Jedda, Harley, Valjoy and Norm. Even Lennie. I knew Lennie wouldn't ever let any Basin Skins break into a camp meant for school kids. I felt so miserable I would have given anything for the sound of my mum's voice. Or even Lennie's. I looked at the time on Margeart's new watch. That watch was really wasted on her as she couldn't tell the time.

It was 1.30 a.m. I didn't think Miss Belmont would give me permission to use the common-room phone so late, so I didn't ask. I sneaked down the corridor and past Barry Hollis where he lay sleeping like a werewolf. He'd been sent to sleep in the common room all by himself, in disgrace for talking after lights out. I tiptoed into the telephone cubicle, shut the glass door and switched on the little light above the phone. I dialled our house number.

When mum finally did answer, she demanded in

a loud panicky voice if I'd broken a leg, if I'd been bitten by a snake, if the camp was surrounded by a ring of bushfires.

'I only rang to chat,' I said.

'You know very well how nervous I am about answering the phone late at night,' she said indignantly. 'I thought it might be that weirdo who rings people up and says he's just poisoned their cat. Not that Norm ever eats anything unless he's pinched it from the kitchen table, and nobody could get close enough safely to poison him, anyway. But the idea, Erk, phoning at this hour! And I went to all the trouble of finding a paper bag and blowing it up ready to bust in his ear over the phone if it was that cat weirdo, and I'm that out of breath now, and it turns out to be only you!'

'ONLY me?' I said. 'If that's the way you feel, I'll hang up. I just thought you might like to hear the sound of my voice after all this time.'

'I heard it only a few hours ago when I saw you off,' mum said crossly. 'And you should be in bed, this hour. What are those teachers thinking of, letting you kids roam around past midnight?'

Behind me in the darkness someone suddenly yanked open the door of the telephone cubicle. I gave a strangled, snorting yelp.

'I'm always telling you, Erk, don't talk with Throaties in your mouth,' mum said. 'They can slide down and get stuck in your windpipe. Gargle with water and get right back into bed. And don't you dare disturb my beauty sleep like this again, and give me palpitations thinking it's someone doing Norm in.' She hung up.

'Barry Hollis, get out of here when I'm making a private call,' I said furiously.

'Who are you ringing?' he asked. 'Your mum?'

'Certainly not! As if I'd be doing anything so immature.' I turned my back on Barry Hollis and spoke into the empty phone. 'I'll give you another ring tomorrow night, Leo, after all the little kids are asleep,' I said. 'And I'll be free on the Saturday when we come back from camp to go parachute jumping with you.' Then I hung up.

'Who's Leo?' asked Barry Hollis.

'Someone I know,' I said. 'You certainly wouldn't know him. And he certainly wouldn't notice you even if you did know him. Anyhow, no one's allowed to use this phone without permission. You haven't got it. You're supposed to be asleep in the common room, in disgrace.'

'Got up to phone my girlfriend,' said Barry. 'I often ring her up at funny hours. She doesn't mind. Get out of the box while I make this call. It's very private.'

I kept a toe in the door to listen. The girl answering Barry's call had a loud cross motherly voice, and she blasted him for ringing at that hour. She wanted to know what the teachers thought they were doing, letting kids roam around after midnight. She told him off for leaving his parka behind when she'd sewn a name label on specially, and she said he'd better be behaving himself up at the camp else she'd belt him one when he got home. Then she hung up.

Barry put the receiver down and came out of the phone box. I didn't want to go back to my room. The long corridor was spookily meshed with shadows, and a tap dripped in the sinister way taps do in the middle of the night. And the thugs were still prowling around on the roof. I wondered if Miss Belmont would mind if I got into her bed.

Barry Hollis's sleeping bag looked like a drowned corpse in the moonlight.

'Bet you're scared, sleeping out here all by your-self,' I said.

'I'm not scared of anything. Not like you, so scared you got up and rang your mum. Some guy named Leo, huh! It was your mum yelling over the phone woke me up in the first place.'

'And your mum yelled just as loud at you, Barry Hollis! Ringing up some girl, huh! As if any girl would let you ring them up in the middle of the night, or any other time. I bet you wanted your mother to drive up here and collect you because you're so scared of the dark.'

'I already told you I'm not scared of anything,' Barry said.

'Oh, aren't you indeed?' asked Miss Belmont coldly.

At the sound of her voice, Barry Hollis and I both jumped into the telephone box and slammed the door, thinking it was the Basin Skins. But when she rapped on the door with her whistle (fancy wearing a whistle with a dressing gown), we had to open the door. She stood over Barry while he meekly got back into his sleeping bag, and then she escorted me personally back to my room.

'It's very unhealthy sleeping with the window shut,' she said severely. She reached over the booby trap and shoved the window up wide enough to let the bunyip from the creek climb in as well as all the Basin Skins. Then she went away, and I lay in bed hating Alison Ashley for not having insomnia.

ELEVEN

In the morning the first thing Margeart said when she woke up was, 'Why are the chairs tied together with a windcheater?'

'It's a temporary clothesline,' I said. 'My windcheater got accidentally wet in the shower, and I had to dry it in case there's a cool change. I hope I didn't wake you while I was doing it.'

'I never wake up once I get to sleep,' said Alison Ashley unnecessarily.

'Neither do I,' said Margeart. 'That's a funny way to dry clothes, Yuk. It looks more like a booby trap for the Basin Skins.'

For such a dumb kid, Margeart Collins could be terribly irritating. Alison was already up and dressed, the clothes from yesterday put neatly into her plastic laundry bag. Wearing a white t-shirt and white jeans, she looked as fresh as a vanilla ice cream. 'Alison, you haven't got the slightest idea about clothes for a school camp,' I said. 'We're going to be bushwalking, not playing lawn tennis.'

'But I never get dirty,' she said.

'That's because you're an only child and you've got your mother running round waiting on you hand and foot,' I said. 'Anyone could look spotless if they're an only child.'

'I happen to look after my own clothes, Erica, and my mother doesn't wait on me hand and foot. You don't know anything about what goes on in our house. Not that it's any of your business.'

I noticed with interest that her expression was changing a little bit, like the surface of a pond when someone tosses a pebble in. I wondered idly what would happen if anyone ever chucked a dirty big rock into Alison Ashley's pond.

Miss Belmont stopped at our door with the terrifying information that she was going to inspect all the rooms in five minutes. 'And by the way, Erica, if you feel homesick in the middle of the night, you're to go and tell Mrs Wentworth,' she said. 'It's extremely thoughtless of you to ring your home and wake up your mother. Especially without having permission to use the phone. In any case, I should have thought a person in grade six quite capable of dealing with a little bout of homesickness.'

Then she went into the next room to paralyse the kids in there with her whistle and clipboard and three-colour snap biro.

The thought of Alison Ashley knowing that I'd babyishly rung up my mum was unbearable. 'I guess you're wondering about the real reason I rang up my house,' I said casually to Margeart.

'No,' said Margeart. 'Did you ring up? But you couldn't have, Yuk. You've been here making your bed.'

'I meant last night,' I said. 'Last night I had this vivid dream about our house burning to the ground with everyone trapped inside, and a newspaper headline with today's date on it. So I had to ring up my place and warn everyone. And it was just as well I did. Mum went round the house checking, and she'd left one of the stove hot plates switched on.'

'Didn't the stove get burnt up with the rest of the house?' asked Margeart, looking puzzled.

'The fire didn't happen, because I warned them in time,' I said. 'Margeart, I wish you'd try to concentrate when people are telling you interesting things.'

'We have a gas stove at our house,' said Margeart. 'Your mum could come over every night and cook on our stove till your house gets rebuilt.'

I gave up.

During room inspection Miss Belmont practically used a magnifying glass and fingerprint powder. Margeart lost points for having a hairpin on the floor underneath her bed, even though it was an old rusty one just about welded to the carpet because it had been there so long. She also lost points for disappearing when inspection was taking place. She must have been mixed up with my talking about fire. She confused room inspection with fire drill, and we found her waiting patiently outside the terrace door, which we'd been told to use if there was a fire at camp. Miss Belmont told her to come in again, but it took a lot of coaxing. Margeart remembered that we'd been told never to go back inside a burning building on any account.

Alison Ashley didn't lose any points. Her bit of the room was as tidy as a museum fossil exhibition. There wasn't one wrinkle in her quilt or pillow, and there wasn't anything on her bedside table except her torch and a polished apple. Miss Belmont gave her ten out of ten.

I didn't score very well at all. I'd forgotten to clean up under my bed after the midnight feast, but Miss Belmont didn't forget to look under there. She pulled out a whole lot of Minty wrappings, silver foil from chocolate, an empty packet of salt and vinegar chips, the wrapping from two Western Waggon wheels, an empty Coke can, and some Throaties with fluff on them. She looked very disgusted, and I felt humiliated. 'All those bits of old paper must have fallen out of my slippers,' I said. 'I always stuff the toes of my slippers with paper to keep them a nice shape.'

'If you must eat during the night, follow Alison's example and keep an apple by your bed,' said Miss Belmont. 'And Erica, stop inventing all those silly excuses. I gave up listening to any of your excuses from the second day of being your grade teacher.'

'Never mind, Yuk,' said Margeart when Miss Belmont went striding off to X-ray all the other rooms. 'I always like listening to your excuses.'

'So do I,' said Alison. 'I think Erica's excuses are always original.'

'Are you insinuating that I tell lies, Alison Ashley?' I demanded.

'I didn't say that at all.'

'You don't have to. I can always tell exactly what you're thinking even though you have that face on all the time.'

'What face? I can't help my face.'

'It's an irritating one, if you want to know. I'm fed up with you looking down your nose just because you happen to live in posh Hedge End Road with an automatic dishwasher and a colour co-ordinated laundry.'

'And I'm fed up with you calling me a snob,' said Alison. 'How can I help where I live, anyway? I have to live where my mother does. You're the one who's a snob, always trying to shut me out of things. Just because you went all through Barringa East Primary and I didn't, you act as though you own it or something. The dark-room and the sick bay and everything. I thought you'd maybe different away at this camp, but you're not. You're just as nasty and bad tempered as ever. It's like sharing a room with a piranha.'

'Don't you dare call me a piranha, you rotten little goldfish!'

'Are you two having a fight?' Margeart asked.

'Of course not,' Alison Ashley and I both said haughtily, not looking at each other.

The breakfast bell rang and after breakfast we had to go into the common room for our first group activity. Miss Belmont gave us a lecture about doing the right thing by Mrs Wentworth.

'The drama programme is going to be handled differently this year,' she said. 'At previous camps some people just sat back and expected the teachers to do all the work. Well, that's not my idea of a school camp at all. We're not going to use those old plays from last year, though I expect a lot of you thought you'd just be handed a script without any effort needed on your part. You can use your activity time this morning to think of an original idea for yourselves. The play can be about anything, but I certainly don't wish to see any violence or anything in poor taste that will give Barringa East Primary a bad name. Mrs Wentworth will be here purely to supervise. If you all work together, you'll gain much more from the Friday drama night as a result. Yes, Erica, what is it?'

It was outrageous! I thought of all the time I'd spent studying the leading roles in order to make a brilliant, dazzling stage debut. 'Can't we use bits out of last year's plays?' I asked. 'We could jumble up the speeches and make two brand-new plays. Couldn't we do that?'

'Certainly not. I want you people to use some initiative. Anyone who doesn't feel like joining in may pack their suitcases and I'll phone Mr Nicholson to come up and collect them.' She left, swinging her whistle by its chain like a knight swinging a mace.

Mrs Wentworth sat down cosily in one of the hard plastic chairs, making it seem almost like an armchair, and got on with knitting her son's cricket jumper.

'Kangas won't ever get a play written by this Friday or any other Friday,' said Jason, who was our group leader. 'Mrs Wentworth, can you write plays?'

'I've never tried to, dear,' she said. 'Knit one through back loop, purl two, cable six. Anyhow, Miss Belmont wants it to be all your own work. Knit two, purl five. There are plenty of nice stories you could adapt for a play. Knit two, purl two, knit one, purl one eight times. What about *Robin Hood and his Merry Men?*'

Even Alison Ashley flinched. 'I guess we'll come up with something ourselves,' said Jason. 'Anyone got any ideas?'

'The Boston Strangler,' said Barry Hollis. 'Jack the Ripper. Bags me being Jack.'

'She said no violence,' Jason said. 'Jeez, you kids, come on, will you? Ideas!'

'We could put on a mannequin parade or a beauty contest,' said Diane, and everyone gave her such a hard time she flounced out on the terrace to sulk. Mrs Wentworth put aside her knitting and went along to coax her back, saying, 'There now, dear, they didn't really mean it. Put a nice big smile on your face and come along and join in the fun.' None of the other Barringa East teachers ever said anything as gooey as that, but because it was Mrs Wentworth, Diane allowed her cheeks to be patted dry and came back again sucking a jelly bean from the store Mrs Wentworth always carried in her handbag.

Our group was having difficulty welding itself into a team. Barry Hollis got bored and went out onto the terrace to trap lizards. 'Barry Hollis nicked off,' Diane said nastily.

'So?' said Jason.

'So you're supposed to be the group leader and keep everyone together. Rehearsing a play, what's more.'

Jason went nervously out onto the terrace, looking as though he didn't enjoy being group leader right then, but Barry came back quietly because he'd found a skink. He sat on the floor and stroked it gently with the tip of his little finger, as loving and tender as a new mother. I stared at him with surprise.

'Let's have a hold of it,' said Paul Kovak, but Barry Hollis didn't say yes or no, he just bunched up the fist that didn't have the lizard in it, and let fly.

'Don't make such a fuss, Paul,' Mrs Wentworth said soothingly. 'I'm sure Barry didn't hit you on purpose. Here, have a black jelly bean while I go and find some ice cubes.' Jason looked as cheerful as a captain going down with his ship. Colin was the only one trying to help with the rehearsal, but all he was doing was arranging the chairs like an auditorium and running along the seats in his football boots. Mark and Lisa and Narelle were over in a corner playing poker. Christine and Diane were picking an armful of bracken and fern and making themselves skirts. Craig was up on the roof. Howard had Margeart Collins guillotined in the window but she hadn't realized yet. Leanne was writing her third letter to her mum. Daryl was drawing felt-pen snake-bite punctures on the calf of his leg.

'Can't you think of something?' Jason asked Alison Ashley.

'I've been trying to, but I just can't,' she said. 'Why don't you ask Yuk?'

I knew very well she said that just to put me in a spot. 'As a matter of fact,' I said triumphantly. 'I have a very good idea for a play. Paul's black eye gave it to me. The play could be set in a hospital. With an operating-theatre scene, and I could buy some sausages and kidneys and liver and stuff to make it look realistic. And we'll have nurses and doctors and a visitor coming in drunk from a football match ... Naturally the matron will be the main part. And naturally, I'll act that, seeing I'm doing all the work thinking up these ideas.'

To my surprise, I discovered that thinking of ideas for a play was easy. Jason yelled at everyone to start rehearsal. Everyone said 'Garn!' but only automatically, the way kids always do when someone suggests a name for a new fish in the classroom tank, or stuff like that. They were relieved someone had finally come up with a better suggestion than *Robin Hood and his Merry Men* or a beauty contest.

'The costumes will be easy,' I said. 'Alison Ashley's brought along enough white clothes to outfit a hospital, and everyone's got pyjamas. Shove some chairs together to look like a row of hospital beds.' While they were doing that, my pencil raced down one foolscap sheet, covered the back of it, attacked another, and I finished Scene One. The matron did most of the talking.

I hadn't actually met a matron, but I'd met a ward sister, when we visited Lennie in hospital after he fell out of his truck and fractured both his legs. The truck wasn't even moving at the time. He'd pulled up by the side of the road so he could listen to the Urquhart Welter Handicap without any distractions, and when his horse came in first at twenty to one, Lennie was so excited, he fell out. Usually people break one leg at a time, but Lennie always overdid things.

Mum made us visit him in hospital, which I found embarrassing in case the hospital staff thought I was related to him. Having his legs immobilized didn't make him less noisy or uncouth. The Sister told him off for bellowing, 'OY, LOVE!' up the ward instead of pressing the buzzer next to his bed when he needed anything. Also for the illegal off-course betting shop he was running at the hospital. So during that visit I'd had the chance to study a ward sister. And matrons would be like that, only more so; in fact, very much like Miss Belmont but dressed in starched white.

I put down my pencil. 'Right,' I said. 'The rehearsal can start. Some of you hop up on the chairs and be patients, and some of you stand around being nurses and doctors. And then I come on as the matron making a tour of inspection. She's a very bossy matron. Everyone has to shake with terror when she runs her fingers along things checking for dust. And she ticks people off for having too many visitors. This is the way the part of the matron should be acted.'

My stage debut; the moment I'd been waiting for since the day I was born!

I sailed out into centre stage. (Probably nobody else in the grade knew that word; they would have said 'the middle of the common room'.) I opened my mouth and began my dazzling career as an actress.

And it lasted maybe sixty seconds, maybe less.

All attention was focused on me, Erica Yurken, centre stage.

And I was swamped by the worst imaginable panic and terror. I gulped in air and licked my lips, but they moved as creakily as though I'd just had enough local anaesthetic injected for a dentist to work simultaneously on every tooth in my head. But not one word came out – just this peculiar honking sound.

'There's nothing funny about swallowing a fly,' Mrs Wentworth reproved the other kids. 'It's a horrible sensation. You've gone quite pale, Yuk, dear; sit by the open window for a minute.'

I stuck my head out of the window into the fresh air and tried to deal with the devastating situation. At home in front of the mirror, I could act. I'd always taken it for granted that I would stroll on stage one day and astound everyone with talent. And instead, I was hanging out of the window like a wet rug and listening to the others rehearsing.

It didn't go very well. They had only a couple of scribbly foolscap pages of dialogue, and all the other fantastic ideas for the play were still bouncing around inside my head. They fought about who was going to play what, and who was going to stand where. Diane Harper wanted to be a disco dancer who had come in with sore feet, and when the doctor fixed them up she would do a solo dance. Everyone yelled at her, so she ran out on the terrace to sulk and Mrs Wentworth had to go and coax her back again.

None of them could think of any good hospital jokes, except Barry Hollis. And even Mrs Wentworth paused in her knitting when he told it. 'That's quite enough, Barry,' she said indignantly, not even calling him 'dear'. 'That sort of joke belongs in a hotel bar.'

'That's where I heard it,' said Barry.

It was unbearable listening to my play being mangled and studded with questionable jokes.

'Aren't you feeling better yet?' Jason demanded. 'We can't read your writing and no one knows what to do next or what to say or anything.'

I left the window and sat in the middle chair in the front row. 'What's needed is a director,' I said. 'We'll leave out the part of the matron for the time being.' And my voice worked perfectly while I read out everyone's lines and told them what to do. I even managed to get Barry Hollis down out of the chimney and onto the stage.

'Who says I'm acting in any dumb play?' he jeered.

'I say so. I wrote this play, and I should know whom to give parts to. If you don't take the part of the drunk visitor coming in from the football match, I'm going to have to cut it right out. There's no one else loud-mouthed and grotty enough to act it except you.'

Barry Hollis took that as a compliment, and oddly enough, he didn't fool around. He learned the words off by heart after only a few attempts, and was really good in the part. That stunned the others into trying harder.

'I reckon this play's going to be all right,' Jason said. 'Let's do it again from where the matron comes in. Only you can't just sit there in the chair reading it. It's too confusing.'

I immediately stopped feeling capable and energetic. Once more the Kangas became an audience. 'I can't be expected to write this play and direct it and do every little job single handed,' I said quickly.

'I'm going to need a temporary stand in. Someone else will have to act the part of the matron during rehearsals till I've got the whole thing worked out. I'll take over on Drama Night, of course.'

'Alison, then,' said Jason.

'I couldn't act a big part like the matron,' Alison said. 'Even if it's only during rehearsals. I've never done any acting in my life. I'd feel embarrassed.'

Fantastic! I hoped that the same panicky stage fright would engulf her, too, and she wouldn't be able to pretend she'd swallowed a fly. Not even Mrs Wentworth would believe that twice. 'There's no need to be embarrassed,' I purred in a fairy-floss voice. 'This is what the matron has to say: "I'm here to make my ward inspection. Nurse Jackson, what is this patient doing on the floor? How dare you leave patients lying around untidily like that during visiting hours! Kindly put him back into bed this minute." Only of course you have to put in a lot of expression and actions and everything. Go ahead, Alison, there's absolutely nothing to it.'

'I've never acted before,' she said humbly. 'Can't I just be a patient like Margeart?'

'It doesn't matter how stupid you sound reading out this part now,' I said, 'because it's not going to be you doing it on Drama Night. I'll be acting it then. Hurry up, we're all waiting.'

Alison, for the first time since I'd known her, looked flustered. Something terrible is going to happen to you in public, Alison Ashley! I thought triumphantly.

Alison self-consciously opened an imaginary door and walked onstage. 'I am here to make my ward inspection,' she said. 'Nurse Jackson, what is this patient doing on the floor? How DARE you leave patients lying untidily around like that during visiting hours! Kindly put him back into bed THIS MINUTE!'

Word perfect! Without even a script in her hand, memorized just from me gabbling it at her once. Voice perfect, too, loud and clear and filling the whole common room and making us all jump. And the actions just right, the walk and everything. I blinked, and of course there wasn't a real hospital matron standing there, just Alison Ashley, the rat, who'd pretended she couldn't act and hadn't ever done any in her life. Just so she could put on a sneaky, brilliant performance like that and make me feel a fool!

'Did I say it right?' she asked.

'Not bad,' I muttered.

'What do you mean, not bad?' Jason demanded. 'She was fantastic! This play's going to be a knock-out on Drama Night, with Alison acting the matron!'

'She's only the understudy!' I said fiercely. 'I thought I made that clear. I'll be the one acting that part on Drama Night!'

'Yes, sure, Yuk,' said Alison Ashley.

Her face was as innocent as a bonneted face in a pram, but I didn't let it fool me for one minute!

* * *

After rehearsal we had free time until next activity session. Everyone clawed biscuits hungrily out of the tin Mrs Wentworth fetched from the kitchen, as though they hadn't eaten for a month. Alison Ashley nibbled daintily at an apple, which she'd washed under the tap for about five minutes. I thought of how the Queen gave Snow White a poisonous apple, causing her to fall into a deep coma. I wished that something like that would happen when Alison bit into her apple, or that at least she'd come across a worm.

Margeart Collins asked me to play table tennis with her on the terrace. Neither of us were exactly championship material. I picked up a bat and served Margeart the ball. She missed and we had a long hunt in the lantana bushes down her end. Then she served and I missed and we had another long hunt in the lantana bushes down my end. Then I served and the ball pinged straight up to the awning and got stuck in the electric-light fitting.

After that it was time for bushcraft with Mr Kennard. He didn't seem to be all that expert at it, really. He had a little paperback book, with a Barringa Regional library sticker on the cover. It was titled *Bushwalking and Camping: a basic safety guide for beginners*, and he kept sneaking it out of his pocket and looking up things when anyone asked questions.

In the free time after lunch I sat on my bed and finished writing the hospital play. I wrote *Curtain* under the last line and clipped all the pages together with a clothes peg. It looked messy, but I couldn't have felt prouder if Mrs Orlando herself had typed it all up on her new electric golf-ball typewriter. While I was reading it through for the tenth time, Wendy Millson, the group leader of Dingoes, stuck her head in through the window.

'Yuk, they said you wrote a terrific play for the Kangas,' she said, crawling like mad.

'Just a knack,' I said. 'I often write plays when there's nothing else to do. There's not much to it, really. Anyone can think up an idea for a play.'

'We can't,' said Wendy humbly. 'We tried half the morning. We even had a go at *Robin Hood and his Merry Men*. Couldn't you do us one?'

'I don't know if I could spare the time. As well as writing the play Kangas are putting on, and directing it, I'm going to play the leading role.'

'I'll clean up your room for inspection every single day.'

'It's funny how people at this camp think I've got nothing better to do than write thousands of words just to save them the trouble. It doesn't seem to occur to anyone that I might like to spend my free time playing table tennis.'

'But no one except Margeart Collins ever picks you for a partner because you're so hopeless,' Wendy said tactlessly. 'I mean, you're better at writing compositions than you are at sport, that's what I meant, Yuk. If you help us out, I'll do the kitchen roster when it's your turn.'

It was a nice sensation, having the great Wendy

Millson grovelling at my feet. 'It would be very hard writing anything the Dingoes could put on,' I said. 'With Kangas, we had a whole lot of talented people, with the exception of Alison Ashley. But Dingoes just don't have anyone at all worth mentioning. Just think of Oscar, for a start.'

Once, when I was in the sick bay, Oscar came limping in with a sore knee from playing soccer. Mrs Orlando told him to roll his jeans up so she could have a look, but Oscar couldn't get them past his shins because his legs were so fat. Mrs Orlando felt his knee through his jeans, but she couldn't decide if one was more swollen than the other, since both his knees were the size of cauliflowers. 'I'd better ring up your mother,' Mrs Orlando said, and Oscar agreed. 'Knee injuries shouldn't be neglected,' Mrs Orlando said, and Oscar agreed. 'Will your mother be home if I ring?' she asked, and Oscar said she would. Mrs Orlando went away to get a bit of paper and a biro to write down his phone number. When she came back and asked Oscar what it was, Oscar said they didn't have the phone on at his house. A sort of male equivalent of Margeart Collins.

Dingoes also had Karen, Vicky and Bev, and they were the closest thing to science-fiction cloning you ever met. They all had blonde hair styled the same way, and if they were in a comic strip, their conversation bubbles would contain identical words.

'We've got Karen and Vicky and Bev,' Wendy

said helpfully. 'And they can all tap dance, and they're in the Marching Girls, too.'

'A tap-dancing march,' I said. 'Fantastic. I'm sure that would hold an audience glued to their seats for three-quarters of an hour.'

'There's no need to be like that. You said just now it was easy, dashing off a play.'

'It is when you have an inspiration. And there's nothing inspiring about Dingoes. It's not as though writing a play's as easy as waving a magic wand around in the air . . .'

My right hand twitched, and as though it had a mind of its own, picked up a pen.

'Cinderella,' I wrote on a fresh sheet of paper. 'Cast: Fairy Godmother – Oscar; Three Stepsisters – Karen, Vicky, Bev; Cinderella – Erica Yurken.'

TWELVE

Next morning I rang up home. Mum was over-whelmingly maternal – perhaps she was feeling guilty because she'd yelled at me when I'd phoned before. She told me to hang on while she rounded up Harley, Jedda, Valjoy and Norm so I could say hello to them.

'I can't wait that long,' I said. 'I've got to go to rehearsal. I have the main part in both the plays. I'm a hospital matron in one, and Cinderella in the other.'

'Really, love? Oh, I can hardly wait to come up and watch you Friday night! Just fancy, playing the lead in both plays!'

'Well, there's no one else here who can act,' I said.

'What are you going to do about glass slippers? If I'd known in time, we could have hired a costume from one of those theatre-costume places. I want you to look your best, seeing it's your first stage appearance. I wonder, if I sprayed your old sandals with adhesive and broke up some bottles and stuck the pieces on, would that look like glass slippers? What do you think, love?'

'We have to make our costumes in art and craft. It's part of the camp programme.'

'Well then, you could wrap Gladwrap round your sneakers. Would that look like glass, I wonder? Erk, seeing you're the leading lady, could you wangle us some good seats in front? I'll get Len to buy some flash bulbs for the camera. I just feel so proud, you being in both the plays!'

'It's nothing,' I said modestly. 'See you Friday.'

I gave Wendy the finished script of *Cinderella*.

'Why's your name down in the cast?' she demanded. 'You don't belong in our group. You have to be out doing sport with Kangas.'

'There's no way you could possibly follow that script unless I was here supervising,' I said. 'No one can read my writing, for a start. And I haven't written any of the actions in. I've got to be here in person to show you.'

'I guess so,' said Wendy unwillingly.

'I'm telling you so. While I go down and get my name marked off the roll with Miss Belmont, you make Dingoes put the chairs out of the way in the common room. I'll be back here in a couple of minutes.'

It took longer. Miss Belmont didn't even listen, because she was organizing Kangas into team games on the tennis court. The human body, in my opinion, looks its best glittering with diamonds and stepping into a silver Rolls. Or lying on a velvet couch plucking grapes out of a bunch. Miss Belmont's ideal of physical perfection was different. She thought people looked better wearing cricket pads, tennis dresses, muscles, track suits and zinc cream. And zigzagging sweatily around after a ball.

'Erica Yurken, you're late,' she said. 'Get into line at once.'

'Can I please be excused from sport?' I asked. 'Dingoes are rehearsing this play . . .'

'Dingoes and what they do aren't your concern.'

'I come out in eczema if I touch a netball,' I said.

'There's nothing about eczema on your school medical report.'

'It only started over the weekend. I was going to tell Mrs Orlando when we get back to school so she can write it down on my card.'

'If Mrs Orlando bothered to write down every

143

one of your imaginary ailments, you'd need a complete filing cupboard all to yourself. Now, kindly join Jason's line and stop wasting time.'

Jason didn't look happy at the prospect. We played that demented game where everyone has to take turns out front throwing the ball to a person, and that person throws it back and bobs down. Then we played tunnel ball, and Roa tripped over and got a gravel knee. (Or got sabotaged by Barry Hollis, depending on which side you were on.) Miss Belmont told me to take Roa in to Mrs Wentworth for first aid.

Next to being injured myself, I liked fixing up other people. So I didn't bother Mrs Wentworth. I took Roa (he was very small, skinny and bashful) into the teachers' sitting room where they kept the first-aid box. I filled a bowl with warm water and antiseptic and began sterilizing his knee. He didn't like it very much, but as he didn't know much English, he just sat and fidgeted.

I did a beautiful job on that gravel rash, cleaning it thoroughly with cotton swabs dipped in the antiseptic. In case there were any germs left, I squeezed on a large amount of Medi Creme. Then I covered it with a big square of gauze.

'I go, plizz?' asked Roa in his little flutey voice, but I still had to put on a splint and a knee-to-ankle bandage. I rolled the bandage just so, with each spiral covering exactly two-thirds of the one before, and pinned it neatly in place with safety pins, tucking in the wadding of cotton wool that I'd lined the splint with. It was a really beautiful job and I was very proud of it.

Mrs Wentworth came in to collect her knitting. 'My goodness, Erica, why didn't you call me at once for an injury like that!' she said. 'Oh, poor little Roa, I just wish I could speak his language! Don't you worry, Roa, there's a very good medical centre down at the shopping centre.' She knelt and undid all the bandages so she could have a look herself. 'Really, Erica!' she said. 'It's only a small graze. Why on earth did you use up all that expensive cottonwool? You've used enough for a whole ward full of chickenpox cases.'

Roa was looking puzzled at having his bandages taken off again so soon, but he didn't need any English to respond to Mrs Wentworth's compulsive mothering. Even a small graze, in her eyes, was worth two black jelly beans. While she was fossicking around in her bag for them, I slipped out into the common room to see how they were getting along with *Cinderella*.

They weren't.

I stood on a chair and said that Miss Belmont was coming up in ten minutes to see how much of the play they'd learned, word perfect. Then in the panic-stricken silence, I got them sorted out and standing where they should for the opening scene.

'Wendy's probably explained why I'll be acting the part of Cinderella,' I said. 'It's very hard to write a complete play at a moment's notice so I'm going to have to add speeches as we go along. Also, none of you can read my writing, and that's another reason why I've got to be in it.'

'But not acting Cinderella,' said Karen. 'She's supposed to be real pretty.'

Some people just haven't got any finesse or tact.

'I've got you and Bev and Vicky down to be the three ugly stepsisters,' I said. 'I've made them real twits in the play, so twitty sort of people have to act them.'

(Actually, when you come to think of it, the biggest twit of anyone in that family was Cinderella herself. Fancy sitting around bawling while everyone else went off to a party, and not having the gumption to pinch some of your sisters' gear and take off somewhere on your own and have a good time.)

But I still wanted, more than anything else in the world, to be Cinderella on Drama Night. And the matron in the hospital play as well. I'd be the only kid, ever, in the history of Barringa East to take the leading role in two separate plays at camp.

I thought about my attack of nerves during the hospital play rehearsal, and composed the following list inside my mind: 1) Every actor suffered from nerves and stage fright, 2) It was nothing to worry about at all, 3) Anyone could overcome anything, especially me, Erica Yurken, with my talent, though maybe not Margeart Collins, 4) Being in the same room as Alison Ashley caused yesterday's slight problem, and 5) As she wasn't here, now was a fitting time to begin my dazzling career as an actor.

'You were only supposed to write the play and get us started,' Vicky said aggressively. 'You're not allowed to barge into other people's activity groups. Chuck her out, Wendy.'

'It seems to me,' I said. 'That some people have the idea that I'm handing out valuable scripts of original plays for nothing. Writers usually get paid for their work. Of course, I can take this play back and sell it to next year's grade six, if you don't want it. You can always do *Robin Hood and his Merry Men.*'

Mrs Wentworth came back from mothering Roa and settled down to her knitting. She didn't even notice I was there.

'Let's start,' said Wendy. 'Seeing Yuk did all the writing, and seeing she's giving up sport now to help us, she can be in the play if she wants to. And I'm group leader of Dingoes, Vicky Picone, and every kid in Dingoes better do what I say, otherwise they're not showing the proper camping spirit. Also, I'll belt them one. Go on, Yuk, show us what we have to do.'

So I went out centre stage and started to play the part of Cinderella.

This time I lasted maybe thirty seconds.

'Funny way to start off a play,' said Vicky. 'Just having Cinderella stand there opening and shutting her mouth.'

It's only Oscar and Vicky and Wendy and everyone, I yelled at myself. And Mrs Wentworth, and she's not even looking at you, you fool, she's counting stitches on her son's cricket jumper. So get on with it. Act, damn you!

And . . . instant laryngitis.

I fled to the security of the director's chair.

'It would be too much of a hassle, acting a big part like that and having to direct and show everyone what to do as well,' I said. 'So I've decided to put the good of the play first. Wendy, you'll just have to be Cinderella.'

And I found again, that when I didn't have to act, I had no trouble at all demonstrating how each line should be said. After a little while they got really enthusiastic, and I could see that maybe the play wasn't going to be too bad at all on Drama Night, if they learned their words in time.

And all without me acting one single line. It just wasn't fair!

Miss Belmont came storming up from the tennis court, with her eyebrows raised vertically to meet her fringe. She came to find out why I hadn't shown up for the rest of the ball games, when Roa had got back ages ago with black jelly-bean syrup around his mouth. 'I was under the impression that I put your name down with Kangas,' she said. 'It's very puzzling, finding you here with the Dingoes activity group. Vicky Picone, is Erica Yurken in Dingoes?'

'No, Miss Belmont,' said Vicky.

'Shane Corbet, is Erica in Dingoes?'

'No, Miss Belmont,' said Shane Corbet.

'Wendy Millson, is Erica in Dingoes?'

'No, Miss Belmont,' said Wendy.

'Well, Erica, are you a member of the Dingoes activity group?' Miss Belmont demanded.

Luckily, just then Miss Lattimore called for Kangas to go over to the hall for art and craft. The dining tables were covered with tissue paper, dowel rods, string and pots of glue. Miss Lattimore said we all had to make kites, but she didn't seem all that enthralled herself. She went and stretched out on a bench under the window and sunbathed in a pair of shorts. She was reading an arty magazine called *Middle Earth*, which was printed on recycled paper. Art and craft teachers always wear very weird clothes. Miss Lattimore wore a peculiar top made out of a hessian bag, with wooden beads threaded through the fringes, and so many handcrafted rings that her fingers looked like quoit stands. Her sandals were weird, too, made of dried seaweedy stuff, decorated with varnished starfish.

Margeart ruined her kite straight off, by cutting the two sticks the same length, so she ended up with a square kite. Miss Lattimore wasn't thrilled at having to get up from her sunbathing to sort it out. 'You're supposed to be using your own initiative while you're at this camp,' she said.

'Can't we make costumes for our play instead of dumb old kites?' Diane grumbled.

Alison Ashley obviously didn't want to make a kite, either, but she was more tactful about it than Diane. 'There are too many people round the tables, Miss Lattimore,' she said. 'I don't mind waiting for a turn. While I'm waiting, Miss Lattimore, do you think I could use the time to run up a few little props and costumes for the play we're doing?'

Miss Lattimore smiled at her and said certainly, and even found a big roll of white butcher paper. Alison Ashley rolled out the paper on the floor and flicked open a pair of scissors. And in no time at all she'd made this fantastic apron and veil. They were just joined up with staples and sticky tape, but when she tried them on, she looked like a real nursing sister.

Then she cut out a pair of spectacles from black cardboard and put them on Jason and changed him into a doctor. Even Miss Lattimore stopped reading her magazine article on 'How to Make Handcrafted Leadlight Letterboxes'. Alison made a neat stethoscope for Jason to wear in the play, and fever charts to pin up on the hospital beds. You could tell that Miss Lattimore was going to give her ten out of ten for craft activity and initiative.

Diane Harper had been sneakily copying, and was making a nurse costume, too, but being Diane, it turned out looking more like a Playboy Bunny without the ears. Alison's, however, was beautiful.

'Talk like the matron,' the kids in Kangas said. 'Go on, say a few words and show Miss Lattimore.'

Alison delivered not only the opening speech, but all the lines belonging to the matron in the whole play. Somehow she'd managed to decipher my untidy script and learn all the lines. She was word perfect, her costume was perfect, she was totally, heartbreakingly perfect for the part.

'Be careful taking off your costume,' Miss Lattimore said. 'It's much too good to damage in any way. Don't rip it.'

I concentrated very hard on tying black paper bows along a kite string. After a funeral in the old days people used to tie black material to their doors to show they were in mourning.

'It's not my costume,' said Alison Ashley. 'I made it for Erica. I'm only the understudy.'

But I knew this wasn't my year to break into Show Business.

'Just as well it fits you,' I said coldly. 'I won't have time to act in the play on Drama Night. I'll be too busy.'

THIRTEEN

After the next morning's rehearsal, I phoned my house again. 'I can only talk a minute,' I said when mum answered. 'There's a big queue of kids waiting to use the telephone.'

There wasn't. They were all out on the terrace helping the teachers and the camp manager prise Margeart's arm out of a length of pipe. Margeart had dropped her earring in the pipe, but instead of just shaking it out, she shoved her arm in up to the elbow, although the pipe's diameter was only coin sized and also S-shaped. The camp manager was going through his toolbox to see if he had any metal cutters before ringing the fire department.

The only other kid waiting to use the phone was Alison Ashley. She waited politely in the kitchenette while I made the call, instead of hanging around outside the glass door with her ears out on stalks, as anyone else would have done.

'Erk, love, I can make a nice little tiara for you to be Cinderella in,' mum said, excited as a bride's mother. 'I can make it out of that rhinestone Cleopatra necklace I wear with my emerald-green velvet.'

'Mum . . .' I said.

'And I thought of a way round the glass slippers. Paint your gum boots white and sprinkle that glittery stuff over while the paint's still wet. If you can't buy paint and glitter up there at the camp, Lennie could bring some up in his truck.'

'Mum . . .' I said.

'And the costume for the matron . . . it's all very well for the other kids in the cast to make their costumes out of paper in art and craft, but the star should have something a bit more special. Lennie has a mate whose daughter's a vet's receptionist. I'm sure she won't mind lending you one of her white uniforms. Will Miss Belmont let us make a tape recording of those plays?'

'MUM!' I yelled. 'What I phoned for is to tell you the road up here's in a really bad way. There's been this landslide, and they don't think it's going to be cleared until Saturday morning, even with bulldozers. It's a shame, but I guess there's no hope of you getting through on Friday night.'

'There's been nothing about a landslide on the telly or in the papers,' mum said, surprised. 'Which road, anyhow? There's dozens of ways to get to that camp. As if I'd let a little thing like a landslide stop me from coming up and seeing you act in a play! In two plays, I mean. Which one's first? You know, I was thinking I could cut up my white patio dress and make a nice matron's veil . . .'

'Mum, I've got this really bad sore throat coming on. It feels like pharyngitis. You'd better not come all the way up here, in case they have to put the understudy on instead of me.'

'Just gargle with salt and water,' mum said comfortably. 'It'll take more than pharyngitis to shut you up. Don't you worry, Erk, you'll be right as rain on the night.'

'These plays we're doing are really dumb. They're not worth the long drive,' I said. 'And there might be a really good film on the telly Friday night, which you'll miss out on, as well as running the risk of catching pharyngitis, or maybe it's scarlet fever, and getting a broken axle from the landslide. It's just not worth it, driving all this way. Think of the petrol.'

'Lennie gets petrol cut price,' said mum. 'Anyway, I want to see you Friday night for another reason. Only I don't want to say it over the phone.'

'A pony club's offered to adopt Jedda so I get to have a bedroom to myself at last?'

'That's not a nice way to talk about you little sister. You shouldn't be talking, anyhow. You should rest your voice if you've got a sore throat, though I must say I can't hear any signs of it.'

'It's sore all right. I think Lennie ought to drive up now and get me, so I can be safe at home in case it's my tonsils. I don't want to be stuck up here in the hills having my tonsils out by some doctor I don't even know.'

'Lennie can't come because he's taking me out for lunch today,' mum said smugly, and rang off.

I put the phone back and Alison Ashley came out of the kitchenette to make her call. I went in there and examined my throat hopefully in the metal of the coffee urn. Some people can actually will themselves to become ill. They go into a trance, but I didn't think I'd have time to get into a deep enough trance for scarlet fever or tonsillitis. The kitchenette, like the sick bay at school, had walls made out of old grocery cartons or something similar, because you could hear every word that was said in the telephone box. Probably that's why Alison Ashley had waited in there, to eavesdrop on my private telephone call. How low could a person stoop?

I put my ear up against the wall, but all she was saying was 'But you promised!' Probably her mum had promised to send her $500 pocket money for the camp, but it hadn't arrived yet in the mail.

'But you promised!' said Alison. 'There's going to be supper after, but you needn't stay for that if you can't. Only for the plays. Well, just for the first play, then. The one I'm in. Everyone's parents are coming. Can't you get someone else to fill in for you at the restaurant? Yes, I know, but ... Oh, that's what you always say!'

I heard her put the phone back, so I sauntered casually out of the kitchenette, as though I'd just been in there for a drink of water. But she didn't even notice me. She barged past, and I could see by her face that someone finally had thrown a big rock into the still surface of her pool. She looked upset and angry. Her face had the same expression as my sister Valjoy's, the time I used Valjoy's battery-operated hair curling wand to heat up some soup when the electricity was turned off at our house.

It was a shock to see Alison Ashley looking like that. It was just as much a shock as if you'd been standing by the side of the road waiting to wave respectfully to Royalty, but when they drove past, they suddenly leaned out the coach window and stuck their tongue out and went 'Blaaaaahhh!'

By the time we lined up to go on our hike, her face was tucked inside its blossomy mask. For our daily torture, Miss Belmont made us walk half way across the State to look at a pioneer village and a dam, even though the sky was massed with rain clouds. Barry Hollis, for some reason, tagged along beside me.

'Why don't you ever comb your hair or change your shirt or have a shower, Barry Hollis?' I asked.

'One time I went without a shower for ten days,' he said.

'I wouldn't be at all surprised,' I said coldly.

'The reason I went without a shower for ten days is that there aren't any showers in that charity clothes-collection bin at the garage,' he said. 'Want to hear about it?'

I didn't, but he told me anyhow.

'It was when the truant officer was hanging round after me. So that's why I went and lived in that collection bin for a bit. It's easy, getting through the flap. It's not so bad, either, sleeping in one of those things. Except my brother and his mates used to come round about midnight and chuck stuff in through the flap. Cracked eggs and pongy, rotten bananas, but except for that it was all right. If I couldn't get off to sleep, I used to try on all the gear.'

'Those clothes are meant for poor people,' I said. 'They certainly wouldn't want them if they knew you'd been trying them on. Specially after not having a shower for ten days. And I can't imagine why you think I'll be interested in hearing about your living arrangements.'

'Because I reckon it would make a great play or book. My whole life would make an interesting book. A terrific one. Or a play.'

'The only book your life would make would be for people training to be convicts,' I said sourly. I thought he probably expected me to be taking down notes like a newspaper reporter at a press conference. Alison Ashley was walking at the head of the line with Jason, but she didn't look bored with his conversation. She didn't look as though she had any troubles in the world. Maybe I'd just imagined that telephone conversation.

'That was real interesting, what I told you about the bin,' Barry Hollis said. 'It would make a whole chapter all by itself for your book. Jeez, what's eating you, Yurken? You've got a face like a dog's dinner. I thought you'd be grateful, getting new ideas, and I'll only charge you a dollar for it. Interest 50 per cent if you don't pay up by next Wednesday.'

'I'm never going to write a book about anything you do,' I said crushingly. 'And there's nothing wrong with my face. My face is all right. It's exactly right for films, if you want to know. One day when I was in the city, this man came up to me and he was a film director. He told me my face was exactly right for films, and I wouldn't even need make up on it or anything. He gave me his telephone number. He said to ring when I was old enough to leave school, and he'd give me an acting job in films straight off.'

'Just as well, then,' said Barry Hollis.

'Just as well, what?'

'Just as well you'll get a chance to act in films, seeing you're hopeless on stage.'

There are two possible methods of removing a band-aid. One of them is to ease it off gently, preferably in warm water, taking tender loving care of your poor battered skin underneath.

And the other way is for someone brutal to get hold of an end and RRRRRRIP!

Either way it hurts like crazy.

And Barry Hollis had just got hold of the end of my particular band-aid and ripped, uncovering the hurt underneath. I would never, never be an actress, not ever, and someone had finally put a voice to it, and said it aloud. There was no possible way I'd be appearing in either of those plays on Drama Night. Not even in a walk-on, say-nothing part. I was too scared even to do that. There was no way I'd be making my stage debut, not on that stage at the sixth-grade camp, or any other stage anywhere, ever.

I was hopeless at acting.

I wished that the dam we were going to see would miraculously collapse. Then I could ring up mum and tell her that she couldn't come to Drama Night because the camp was cut off from civilization. But mum would still come, even if she had to find a rowing boat. No matter what, she'd be there, all dressed up in her best outfit. Her best outfit was the colour of apricots when they've got too ripe, and the skirt had hundreds of little accordian pleats and a belt with a large glittery buckle. The top had float-ing sleeves, also accordian pleated, and a huge rose, only it looked more like a cabbage, made out of the same material as the dress. And shoes with glitter-ing heels to match the buckle, and an evening bag to match the shoes. Lennie thought she looked fan-tastic in it.

The other kids would think she looked fantastic, too, because that was the sort of outfit their mothers would think just great. But there was one person I didn't want seeing my mum all overdressed like that, and maybe have a quiet snigger and smirk to herself, and that was Alison Ashley.

And then, of course, there would be Lennie, coming to see me act. He'd probably slap Miss Belmont on the back and say, 'G'day, love, how yer going?'

I thought of all the years I'd been nagging to go to acting lessons and voice training classes, even though I knew we could never afford it, and how I'd boasted to mum on the phone about being picked for the main rôles.

What a great big drippy fool I was going to look tomorrow night in front of everyone!

When we got back from our excursion, Miss Belmont planned a barbecue tea and campfire, as though daring the big plasticine-coloured rain clouds to defy her. She organized Mr Kennard into going down to the shopping centre for sausages. Everyone begged him to bring back packets of chewing gum and icy poles, but he said irritably, 'Can't you kids get through four days at camp without spending money on junk food?'

But when he came back from the shops, he took a whole lot of personal stuff into the teachers' sitting room, and it was the grown-up equivalent of junk food.

While the barbecue was cooking, the Kangas and Dingoes had a rehearsal of their plays in the dining hall, which I couldn't bear to attend. It was too painful to be a spectator. And anyhow, they didn't need me anymore, because they'd finally learned their lines. I rang home instead.

'I'm glad your pharyngitis is all cleared up,' mum said brightly. 'I've been thinking some more about glass slippers. What about if I lined your old transparent plastic sandals with cooking foil?'

'Miss Belmont doesn't want parents having anything to do with the costumes,' I said. 'That's why I'm ringing. Miss Belmont's not all that keen on parents. She thinks they're a nuisance. I get the impression that she really doesn't want this camp littered up with parents on Drama Night'

'Nonsense,' said mum. 'They like the parents to take an interest. As if I'd miss out seeing you in those plays. Jedda won't come, because there'll be show jumping on the telly, and I won't be able to budge Harley out of his hammock, and Valjoy no doubt has other fish to fry, but don't you worry about Len and me not turning up, love.'

'Some kids' parents aren't coming. I don't think Alison Ashley's mother will. She has to work or something.'

'That's really terrible,' said mum. 'I'd just hand in my notice if they expected me to work and miss out seeing you act. Why, Lennie was supposed to be doing the Portland run tomorrow, but he charged into the depot and created a din till they put some other bloke on instead.'

'Did he?' I asked hollowly.

'You bet he did. He wouldn't miss out on your

concert for anything. He was going to order a big floral bouquet, too, and have it delivered to the camp by Interflora, just like they do on first nights in real theatres. But I told him it might make the other kids feel a bit left out. It's not their fault they haven't got your acting talent.'

'Mum,' I said desperately. 'About tomorrow night . . .'

'I've got to go, Erk. Norm's just bailed up next door's German Shepherd. See you tomorrow night, love.'

I put the phone back and went out to the barbecue with no appetite. The campfire didn't last long, anyhow. After we finished eating, Miss Belmont organized us into a circle to sing campfire songs, but it started raining. So she organized an evening of projected colour slides in the common room instead.

While she was setting up the projector, I stared glumly out the window, thinking that there was nothing more depressing than rain. Unless it was Margeart Collin's company.

'It's a disappointing thing about clouds,' Margeart said. 'When we were driving up to this camp, you could see the clouds sitting on top of the mountain, and they looked all white and fluffy. But they're not a bit like that when they come down low and you're in the middle of one. They're just wet and grey like rain.'

'Don't worry about it too much, Margeart,' I said, and moved to another window, but the view there was even more depressing. It looked out on the camp sewerage equipment.

I moved to the last window, and the view there was the most depressing of all. Mrs Wentworth turned the lights on in the common room, and there was Alison Ashley's dazzling reflection in the glass. She'd changed her clothes after the barbecue. She was wearing a white ruffled dress, and her hair was plaited and pinned round her head, like a coronet. Princess Alison Ashley. She looked as though she ought to be sitting at a spinning wheel in a castle tower, instead of helping Miss Belmont set up audio-visual gear.

'Who left this bundle of scrap paper on the table?' Miss Belmont said. 'I need a clear space for the box of slides.'

I went to retrieve the master copies of my two plays. Scrap paper was right. They'd been written on any paper that came to hand, mostly on the reverse sides of Mr Kennard's eucalyptus identification test which everybody flunked except Alison Ashley. My handwriting looked even more terrible than usual, because of all the crossing out and rewriting of dialogue. I wondered if Shakespeare's rough copies had looked any better. Probably a whole lot worse because he had to write with a bird's feather dipped in ink.

There certainly wasn't any point in keeping such a mess. Everyone had copied out their parts and learned them, and I no longer felt any creative pride. I was too depressed about Drama Night.

The whole lot belonged in the wastepaper basket, which is where I put it.

FOURTEEN

While everyone was getting ready for Drama Night, I tried to find twenty cents to make one last desperate phone call home. I'd spent all my pocket money, so I sold Margeart Collins a couple of burnt sticks I'd hastily grabbed from the barbecue. I told her they were authentic Aboriginal fire sticks from the souvenir shop at the pioneer village. Margeart thought they were lovely, and I felt crooked and mean, but intended to buy them back from her when I was financial again.

When I dialled our house, Valjoy answered in the special voice she always used in case it was a boy at the other end of the line. 'Helloooooo,' she purred into the phone.

'It's me. Erk.'

'Oh, it's only you, is it?' she snapped in her normal bossy voice.

'I want to speak to mum.'

'Well, you can't. She and Lennie left early to see you act in that crummy little childish concert. And I don't want to talk to you. I'll be seeing you tomorrow, worse luck, when you get back from camp. Which reminds me, you little creep, tomorrow is when I'm going to murder you for sneaking off with my clothes! I thought I told you . . .'

Her long detailed list of revenges did nothing to raise my spirits, and she hung up only when she ran out of breath.

Some parents were already starting to arrive, so Miss Belmont set them to work arranging the chairs in the hall, to pay them back for coming early. Each time a car drove up, kids would squeal and hang out the window. Alison Ashley looked hopefully at each arriving car, too. Miss Lattimore's boyfriend turned up in a landrover plastered with Conservation stickers. She didn't scream and rush across the carpark to meet him, the way Vicky and Karen did with their visitors, but Miss Lattimore did what I suppose was the adult version. She hurried into her bedroom and came out wearing fresh lipstick and a new weird top, one she hadn't worn at all during the week, and her hair was combed up elegantly and fastened with a hand-crafted leather slide. Then she went out to meet her boyfriend, though she said hello to him round the end of the building, which was hidden from the windows. Everyone was dislocating their necks trying to see what he looked like. I could have told them without even looking; he'd have a beard, long hair caught back with a rubber band, and a folk guitar.

Mrs Wentworth told everyone to hurry up and finish getting into their play costumes and queue up in the common room for her to make up their faces.

She tried to make Alison Ashley look severe by drawing frown lines on her forehead, but they just looked like the bloom on a butterfly's wing. I thought gloomily that Alison would probably go right through life without any wrinkles, crows' feet, middle-age spread, or even acne.

The queue wasn't very stable. Everyone kept charging about with brilliant last-minute ideas – such as, could they take down the curtains in the common room because they dreamed up this great way of making a hoop skirt if Mrs Wentworth had a bale of fencing wire and a sewing machine. Mrs Wentworth was being kind and patient, but even her voice was wearing thin. No matter what part they were playing, everyone wanted a scar running across their cheeks with stitches in it, because that's what Barry Hollis painted on himself.

Diane Harper didn't look one bit like a nurse. She sneaked off and redid her make up after Mrs Wentworth finished. She outlined her eyes in black and gave herself a beauty spot, and looked more like Valjoy on Saturday nights than a hospital nurse.

When Mrs Wentworth sorted out the last face, she raised her voice above the hullabaloo. She said quite snappily that everyone had to sit down and play a nice quiet game such as Cluedo until it was time to go over to the hall to give the concert. She made herself a cup of strong black coffee and went into the teachers' sitting room and shut the door firmly.

I didn't blame her. The kids were silly with excitement. They didn't play Cluedo. They skylarked and giggled and jumped about and fought viciously for the space in front of the mirror so they could admire their faces in greasepaint. Jason and Wendy tried to keep their groups quiet. Wendy threatened that Miss Belmont would hear and ring up Mr Nicholson and he'd come up and drive us straight back to Barringa East.

But it was Jason who had more success. 'Shut up, you kids!' he yelled. 'Can't you even keep quiet for twenty minutes? Practise your lines or something! It's only twenty rotten little minutes to Drama Night.'

As soon as he said that, everyone looked at the big clock over the common-room door and stopped clowning. In the silence, you could hear the people gathered in the dining-hall building. It was a combination of low murmuring and feet being shuffled and polite coughing. A sound of expectant waiting. Kangas and Dingoes stared up at the clock's big hand moving towards Drama Night and suddenly went pale underneath their greasepaint.

And that was when things started to go wrong.

Oscar decided that nobody was getting him up on a stage wearing a dress with two balloons stuffed down the front. He decided, in fact, that nobody was getting him up on a stage as a fairy godmother, and that nobody was getting him up on a stage full stop. He crawled under the table when Wendy

166

Millson tried to pin on his wings. The balloons burst, and they'd been the only ones left in the whole camp.

The *Cinderella* play revolved around Oscar, and there was no one else to take the part of the fairy godmother. I looked at him helplessly, wondering how directors and stage managers dealt with actors who clung to a table leg and refused to go onstage

'I won't be in it, either,' Shane said. 'Not if he's not in it. If he's not in it, we might as well chuck the whole play.'

Then Jason remembered that I'd forgotten to get any suitable meat for the operating scene in the hospital play, and Kangas started to panic. 'We'll have to leave that bit out!' Diane wailed. 'It was the best part! And you've got the nerve to call yourself a stage manager!'

'We might as well ditch our play, too,' Jason said bitterly. 'Everything leads up to that operating theatre scene. Thought you said you'd fixed up all the props, Yurken? You said you'd have them all ready in the carton. Some Drama Night this one's going to be!'

'And where's the pumpkin?' Vicky demanded. 'It's certainly not here in the carton, either. Every rehearsal you said you were going to handle all that! You said you were the director and the producer and the stage manager and everything else!'

'And the glass slippers!' cried Wendy. 'What am I going to use for glass slippers?'

Alison Ashley was the only one who didn't join in the roar of accusations.

'I don't know why you're all panicking,' I said haughtily. 'All the props for this Drama Night have naturally been taken care of. I was just about to go out and collect them.'

I slipped outside and had my own private, personal panic in the carpark.

'How yer going, movie star?' a big voice boomed over my head. 'It's been a quiet old week without you. Your mum's gone ahead to grab some seats down the front, but she sent me over to give you this.'

I opened the lid of the box Lennie gave me, and inside was a wonderful pair of glass slippers. Mum must have sat up all night making them. She'd sewn hundreds of little transparent sequins all over a pair of silver pull-on slippers. The effect was magical.

I burst into tears.

Lennie didn't say anything. He put his arm around me and let me bawl all over his Gold Coast shirt with the hula girls on it. In between bawling I told him all about it; about being dead hopeless at acting, and writing two plays which I'd thought were pretty good when I wrote them but now they seemed just plain dumb and no one wanted to act in them anyhow and the audience would all get up and go home after the first five minutes and it was all my fault. I told him about what a lousy stage manager I was and how I'd forgotten all about the pumpkin and about the balloons bursting and everything and how I'd led mum to believe that I was going to be the star of Drama Night.

Lennie pulled out his hanky and dried my eyes as gently as Mrs Wentworth would have done, and I was so surprised I stopped bawling.

'She'll be apples, love,' he said calmly. 'Let's see now, a pumpkin, two balloons, some snags, and someone to go in there and sort out a kid called Oscar. No sweat. Let's see if anything's fallen off the back of my truck.' He headed towards the hall, and I followed, but he didn't go in the main door. He went round the back to the kitchen, apparently not even bothered by the sign on the door saying that no one was allowed in there except the camp manager. Lennie just went over to the freezer and opened the lid. He searched through the packages and pulled out a plastic bag full of sausages!

'There,' said Lennie. 'There's no kids' camp in the whole country that wouldn't have snags in the freezer. Now, where do they keep the vegies?' He found the cupboard and pulled out a couple of grapefruit. 'These do instead of balloons?' he said. 'There's no pumpkin here, but never mind, there's a watermelon. No rule says you can't have a watermelon in *Cinderella* instead of a pumpkin.'

He started to help me carry it back to the common room, but as we were passing the hall, Miss Belmont stuck her head out the door and said bossily, 'Are you one of the parents? You'll have to

169

come into the hall at once and find a seat. Mr Er. The concert will start very soon.'

Lennie didn't slap her on the back and say, 'G'day, love, how yer going?' He just handed me the watermelon and went meekly into the hall. Luckily Miss Belmont didn't notice me; she was too busy intimidating another lot of parents who had arrived late.

I went back to the common room with my red eyes hidden behind Lennie's driving sunglasses. Everyone calmed down when they saw the sausages and watermelon, even though it wasn't a pumpkin. Wendy went into raptures over the glass slippers. But Oscar stayed put under the table and wouldn't come out.

Wendy and Jason tried out their leadership qualities. I tried flattery and bribery, but Oscar just stubbornly repeated that no one was getting him up on any stage to make a dill of himself. Everyone tried, even Barry Hollis, though that wasn't out of sympathy for the rest of us; he just didn't want to risk the concert being cancelled and miss out on the chance of showing off in front of a whole lot of people. But Oscar didn't even take any notice of Barry Hollis. I thought desperately that I'd have to go over to the hall and somehow get past Miss Belmont and bring Lennie out to deal with Oscar. But the clock said I'd run out of time. There were only four minutes left to Drama Night.

'Yuk, you'll just have to be the fairy godmother,' said Wendy Millson. 'There's nobody else. Hurry up and get those clothes off Oscar. You know all the lines and everything. Well, what are you waiting for?'

I felt as though someone had just clobbered me with a sock full of sand.

'Get a move on,' Wendy said impatiently.

I thought of the packed hall and felt my hands start to shake. I put them in my jeans pockets and hid my panic behind Lennie's sunglasses.

'Stop mucking around, Yuk,' everyone said. 'Miss Belmont will be over in a minute. Get a move on, Yurken.'

'I . . . can't,' I said numbly, and felt my voice dry up in my throat and the shaking spread from my hidden hands down to my knees. Everyone stared at me curiously. The only one who didn't was Alison Ashley. I looked at her carefully, and saw that she knew the reason, and had known it all along. I waited for her to blab it out to everyone, and jeer and scoff, but she didn't do any of those things. Instead, she bent down and grabbed Oscar by the ankles and yanked viciously and at the same time she began yelling. I jumped, and so did everyone else. None of us recognized her voice.

'You come on out of there, Oscar!' she yelled. 'Erica can't possibly get dressed in time and have her face made up. A lot of work went into fixing these two plays. If you go mucking up Drama Night, you'll look like a smear of strawberry jam

171

once I get through with you! I'm going to count to three, and if you don't come out of there by then, I'll tear out your liver and use it for the hospital play!'

It was so amazing to hear Alison Ashley brawling just as loudly and uncouthly as anyone else in Barringa East Primary, that Oscar was too startled to make a fuss. He crawled out from under the table and stood still while I crammed the two grapefruit down the front of his dress. It was just as well he did, because Miss Belmont came over.

'Form two orderly, straight lines,' she said. 'Kangas are on first, so Dingoes may sit quietly down the back of the hall to watch until it's their turn. No unseemly behaviour from anyone. Erica Yurken, where do you think you're going?'

'To my room,' I said. 'I've got a migraine headache.' I needed to recover from the shock of having almost been on stage. I didn't even want to watch those two plays.

'Drama Night is not the time to have migraines,' Miss Belmont said. 'That is not the proper camping spirit at all.' She frowned me into line and we all went over to the dining hall. Miss Belmont took the Dingoes through the back door, and the Kangas went through the side door behind the curtain Mr Kennard had rigged up out of blankets on a wire. Jason and the others began putting the hospital beds made out of chairs and sheets into position. I felt sick enough to crawl into one of them. Jason tucked the sausages up under his shirt for the operation

172

scene, and everyone got into place on the stage. The hum of conversation from behind the curtain stopped as Mr Kennard pulled the wire and the blankets slid jerkily apart.

Alison Ashley drew a deep breath and walked forward to make her entrance as the matron. And her dazzling debut as an actress.

I couldn't stand it. I slipped out of the side door and ran through the darkness to the dormitory block and into my room. Suddenly those two plays didn't seem funny at all. They seemed embarrassing and terrible, and I knew nobody would laugh at the jokes, except maybe Lennie. I just wanted to die, thinking of everyone's parents driving all the way up from Barringa East. Maybe they'd mob Miss Belmont afterwards and demand to be reimbursed for petrol. And after the whole humiliating business was over, I still had to face my mum.

If ever there was a time I'd longed for a burst appendix and an ambulance dash to hospital, it was then. I lay down on my bed and tried to will it to happen. I concentrated for what seemed like hours. I kept my fingers on my ears so I wouldn't have to listen to the booing. The only thing they'd find pleasing about the whole night would be Alison Ashley's acting.

It's difficult, though, to concentrate on anything if you're lying on a book. I became aware that someone had left a book on my bed. I turned on the light and looked at it. It was a hand-made book, stapled into a white cover with the edges bound in gold masking tape. Inside the cover were my tatty old pages of scribbled scripts. Someone had trimmed the ragged edges and put them in order. I looked at the title on the cover for a long time. It was made from gold Letraset, sealed to the cover under a sheet of adhesive plastic so it would last for ever.

'*Cinderella. Barringa East Hospital.* Two plays by Erica Yurken.' That's what the title said.

I never ever thought much about the word 'by'. Such a plain, short word, it gets tucked away inside sentences and lost. It doesn't have the dynamism of words like osteogenesis or gastroduodenostomy. But right then, isolated like that on the cover of a book, it suddenly seemed to me like a blast on a trumpet. Or a red carpet spread out on a footpath. Or maybe even the sound of hands clapping in a darkened auditorium.

There was only one thing wrong with the cover, and it had nothing to do with Alison Ashley's beautiful painstaking handwork. It was my name, Erica Yurken. If I was going to be a playwright, I'd most certainly have to change it, but I'd have to think about that later.

Right then I had an opening night to attend, even though I'd missed most of it.

When I sneaked in the back door of the hall, Miss Belmont turned around and shot me a chilly look, not at all the sort of look that usherettes ought to bestow upon playwrights. There were some vacant seats down among the parents and visitors, but there was another empty seat in the back row where Kangas were sitting. It was next to Alison Ashley. So I sat there. *Cinderella* was almost finished. They'd reached the part about the glass slippers. It wasn't too bad at all. In fact, it was a credit to the cast, producer, director and stage manager.

Everyone clapped like mad when it ended. I thought it would look conceited if I did, so I looked modestly down at my book. Then I looked sideways at Alison Ashley, and found that she was looking sideways at me. I opened my mouth to say this dignified speech of thanks I'd prepared coming over to the hall, but somehow I couldn't get the words out. There was a lot of distracting noise going on, anyhow. Oscar had to come out and take a bow all by himself, and some grown ups in the audience were stamping their feet and whistling and carrying on. Miss Belmont was frowning at them as though she wished she could order them all to pick up papers in the playground at recess as a punishment.

So what I said instead was, 'Thanks a lot for the book. It's great.'

'That's okay,' said Alison Ashley. 'I couldn't stand seeing those scripts end up in the wastepaper basket.'

I could hardly hear her over all the noise and the clapping. Lennie's voice was louder than anyone's. And I suddenly realized what he was shouting. 'Author!' he was yelling out. 'Author!'

I felt myself turning bright red.

'Go on,' Alison said in my ear. 'Get out the front, Yuk, up on the stage.'

I didn't want to. I clamped my fingers round the back of the chair in front, but Alison Ashley unhooked them one by one and shoved me out into the aisle. I stood there, staring down at my shoes. Then Alison Ashley, traitor to the last, even though we'd just that minute been smiling tentatively at each other, called out, 'She's down here!' And not only that, she set her hand in the small of my back and pushed me up the aisle and up the stairs onto the stage. With her other hand gripping the waistband of my jeans so I couldn't nick off.

There was all this clapping, and Lennie yelling out 'Author! Author!' and other people copying him, and I didn't know where to put myself. I couldn't gawk at my shoes for ever, so finally I had to look out at that audience, and it was terrible! Was I glad I didn't have to be a professional actor and face that six nights every week! And last of all I glanced guiltily down at my mum, but she didn't look one bit disappointed. Her eyes were bright with pride. And I was so happy she'd come. I ached with gratitude that I was me, and not Alison Ashley, whose mother hadn't bothered to turn up at all.

Then Jason and Wendy came onstage and made a speech on behalf of grade six, thanking the camp manager for the nice meals, and all the teachers for giving up their free time so we could go to camp. (It wasn't Jason and Wendy's idea, that thank you speech; Miss Belmont had told them earlier that as group leaders they had to.) Then they presented the gifts we'd all bought with our pocket money, though Miss Belmont hadn't told us we had to, that was our own idea. The camp manager was given a soup ladle, Miss Belmont a new whistle, Mr Kennard a compass, Mrs Wentworth a king-sized packet of black jelly beans, and Miss Lattimore a crafty pendant made out of resin with a dead bee in it.

After that was all over, the parents put the seats back around the hall ready for supper. Miss Belmont told me and Alison to tidy up the stage, so we wouldn't get swollen heads, me for being the resident playwright, and Alison for being such a hit in the hospital play, which I'd stupidly missed out on seeing.

While we tidied away the props from the stage, we found Margeart Collins. She was still in the makeshift bed being a hospital patient. The cast of *Cinderella* had shoved the bed to one side behind the curtain while their play was on, but Margeart hadn't realized yet that Drama Night was over. She was lying still with her eyes shut, as I'd trained her to do during all the rehearsals.

I poked at her and she opened her eyes and sat up. 'Oh, good,' she said. 'I'm glad it's all over. Acting's very tiring.'

'You can go and get yourself some supper, Margeart,' I said. 'Your mother's looking for you, anyhow.'

Mrs Collins wasn't, she was having a long discussion with Miss Belmont about all the clothes and possessions and school equipment Margeart had managed to lose during the week at camp. Margeart took one look at them both and got back into bed. She had her cluey moments

'You'll have to get off this stage so Alison and I can clean up,' I said firmly. 'If you don't want to talk to your mum just now, go and chat to mine.'

'She's busy talking to her boyfriend,' Margeart said. 'I could go and talk to Alison's mother instead. Which one's her?'

Alison Ashley's face went still.

'Alison, where's your mum?' Margeart persisted

'Mrs Ashley isn't here tonight,' I said. 'She's an air-traffic-control technician, and airports can't close down just because there's a concert on.'

Margeart looked very impressed, and went away to get herself a lamington and tell people that someone's mother was going to be arriving late by helicopter.

Alison went on putting the stage props back into the carton. I carefully didn't look at her. 'Listen,' I said. 'Your mum might have started to drive up here and found a big tree fallen across the road.'

Alison didn't say anything.

'She might have started to drive up here and found an injured Saint Bernard dog by the road and turned round and taken it back to the animal hospital,' I said.

Alison silently folded Oscar's fairy godmother wings and put them into a box.

'She might have had a very good reason,' I said. 'Maybe she couldn't phone and tell you what it was because there was a gale-force wind and all the power lines are down in Hedge End Road.'

'It isn't because of that at all.' said Alison. 'She didn't turn up for the same reason she never does; because she's not interested in anything I do. She won't even be there at school tomorrow to meet the bus.'

I looked down at my mum in her apricot outfit. She looked terrific.

'How are you getting your suitcase back to your place then?' I asked Alison.

'Same way I got it to school when we left for camp. I'll manage. It's only a five-minute walk.'

'Lennie's coming with Mum to pick me up. We'll give you a lift.'

I waited for her to say that she wouldn't be seen dead driving round in a truck with someone like Lennie, but what she said was, 'Thanks, Yuk, that'd be great.' Then she looked at me and grinned. 'Lennie's got time off tomorrow, has he, from being a security guard at your mansion over near Kyle Grammar School?'

'All right then, smarty,' I said. 'He's not a security guard at all. He's a trucky.'

'No, he's not,' said Alison. 'You can do better than that. He's a circus acrobat who broke his collarbone and your mum's nursing him back to health seeing she used to be a bare-back rider in that same circus and that's where they met.'

'Or a ballet dancer and he wears his shoes with the ribbons criss-crossed up to his knees,' I said.

'And he's got tomorrow off because he had to have a fitting for his pale-blue *Swan Lake* costume.'

Mum, who had got sick of beckoning to me (only I pretended not to see because I was too embarrassed to face her), charged up the steps onto the stage in a swirl of apricot-coloured accordion pleats, and flung her arms around me. 'Erica, you're sly!' she said. 'Letting me think you were going to be acting like the other kids, and all the time you were in charge of writing those two plays! I never knew you could write! You could have knocked me over with a feather when Lennie told me just before the curtain went up.'

So I stopped feeling embarrassed and felt proud instead. I showed her my book and she straightaway wanted to send it special delivery to a gardener Lennie knew who worked at one of the television channels to pass it on to the management.

'Not this copy,' I said. 'This copy's sort of special.'

Then mum told me her good news. She and Lennie were getting married, and they were going to announce it at a surprise party tomorrow night. I looked down at Lennie, being made to pass cups of tea around by Miss Belmont. He looked nice in his Gold Coast shirt with the hula girls on it, and I hoped mum would let him wear it to the wedding.

'Alice, do you want to come to our party tomorrow night, love?' mum said. 'You'd be very welcome.'

180

'Her name's Alison,' I said. 'Mum, I wish you'd remember my friends' names.'

Alison said she'd like to come to the party, and I said off-handedly that if she wanted to stay the night she could, if she didn't mind sharing a bedroom with a horse. Alison said she'd love to.

Miss Belmont wasn't letting anyone linger over supper. She went around the hall briskly taking cups away from people who hadn't finished yet, then she organized team games and bullied the parents into joining in. An hour later she finished the last game and all the parents fell into the nearest chairs choking for breath. Miss Belmont didn't let them stay there. She thanked them for coming to Drama Night, and said they'd better go home now, and not hang around being a nuisance, as we had to get up early to tidy up the camp. She didn't use those exact words, but that's what she meant.

Alison and I said goodbye to mum and Lennie at the car, then we walked over to the dormitory block. Alison said as it was the last night of camp, I could borrow her kimono if I wanted. So I let her borrow Valjoy's black transparent nightie which Miss Belmont hadn't noticed when she put everything else into that plastic bag.

I hung the kimono up where I could look at it while I had my shower. I propped the book under the kimono, so I could look at it, too. I realized with immense, sudden joy, that I had a chance to get rid of my awful surname. If mum was changing hers, maybe I could, too. Sometimes kids did, if their mothers remarried. Erica Yurken sounded absolutely terrible for a playwright. I could take Lennie's surname, now he was going to be my stepfather.

I thought about that. And yelped.

'What's the matter, Yuk?' Alison called from the next shower cubicle.

'Grubb!' I howled. 'Lennie's last name is Grubb!'